THE HIDDEN TRUTH ABOUT
BROKEN SUGAR BOWLS

LAROUNA PINCKNEY-MAYBIN

Order this book online at www.trafford.com
or email orders@trafford.com

Most Trafford titles are also available at major online book retailers.

Cover art by Larouna Pinckney-Maybin

All biblical scripture quotes were taken from the King James Version of the Bible.

Print information available on the last page.

ISBN: 978-1-4907-8980-4 (sc)
ISBN: 978-1-4907-8982-8 (hc)
ISBN: 978-1-4907-8981-1 (e)

Library of Congress Control Number: 2018950739

Trafford rev. 07/19/2018

 www.trafford.com

North America & international
toll-free: 1 888 232 4444 (USA & Canada)
fax: 812 355 4082

Table of Contents

1969-2013

This book is written in memory of my sister Albertina Sherrod (rest in peace big sis) and my son Elaundre Foster (I miss you Baby Boy). Although your time here has ended my love for you will never. Until we meet again I love you both.

1998-2016

Acknowledgements

First and fore most giving honor to God through which every success in my life has been made possible. Special thanks to all the strong women of the world especially those whom I've had the privilege of learning how to be a strong woman. Thanks to all those who believe in me. To my family, friends, and advisors; I thank God for you and may heaven smile upon you always. Special thanks to my mother Rosetta McMillan-Clifford aka Rose Dean who encouraged me to keeping writing and inspiring me to continue to do what I have a passion for. I love you all.

Introduction

T*he Truth About Broken Sugar Bowls* is a series of short stories that depict the lives of some fictional characters that endure real life situations. These stories are reminders of how sweet life may be one minute and disastrous the next. *The Sweet Payback* offers a sense of customary reading about how life may appear to be predictable. However, there is a shocking twist that leaves the reader scratching their head in astonishment that life is not always the way it appears to be. *The Life of Rose Dean* is a short story of true events that have occurred in the life of my mother. The story is about recalled thoughts of a single "*strong*" woman bearing and raising 21 children alone. *The Force of Life's Confessions* is a previously released story about the assumptions of a woman with trust issues that has a tragic and cliff hanging ending. *I Should Have Known Better* is the sequel and ending of *The Force of Life's Confessions*. *Cracked Bowl* is a story about a woman who fights to remain in a toxic relationship until she meets a man who changes everything.

fog of lust and desire in the women for him. No woman could refuse him. He thought that every woman he inveigled (enticed) would fall in love with him and submit to his every command. Julius was smart and business savvy. He was part owner of a profitable temp agency that he and his partner started 15 years ago. He only spoke of Mr. Smith when asked about how the business came to be. He stated that he met Mr. Smith and they became fast friends when he and his wife vacationed in Bali. After they exchanged numbers, held meeting with lawyers and financial advisors their business venture came to fruition. It was late Friday morning, and one of the busiest days of the week for the temp agency. Julius had the daunting task of assigning temp logs to the 4 desk clerks and ensuring that workers were going out as soon as the logs were coming in. Three of the women in his office he had affairs with during some point in his marriage. As he began making his rounds through the office; in walks a tall slim distraught young lady with long legs and disheveled hair. "Hello," she states as she approached the front desk. "I am here to inquire about a job I saw on your website posting for an office staffer at a pay rate of $17.23." "Is that job still available?" Julius did a 180-degree turn. He wanted to see the face of the woman he had already presumed to be his next victim. "Hello, my name is Julius." "How may I help you?" He flashed his infamous smile. Although, he had two crooked teeth in the front of his mouth and one missing on the bottom he always smiled as if he had a mouth full of pearly whites. He stood dazed imagining all the ways he wanted to alter the young lady's life. His thought was quickly interrupted when the receptionist in the front cubicle called his name. "Mr. Kindle, your wife is holding on line 3." In his mind he screamed; "dag nab it!" "Excuse me," he stated to the mysterious woman as he stepped back and turned to walk the 70 feet stretch down the hall to his office to take the call from his wife Elisabeth of 15 years. "Mandy get Ms… ah, I'm sorry I didn't get your name?" "My name is Mrs. Silva," "Brianna Silva," she stated. "Ok, Mandy will you get Mrs. Brain the Silver;" he stated to get a reaction from mocking her name. "Get Mrs. Brain the Silver an employment intake packet and get her started with the paper work." "If I'm not back in 20 minutes, please begin the screening process without me." Without so much as a blink Brianna looked at Julius and then down at the packet of papers which seemed to contain at least 20 pages. "Excuse me," she managed to assertively interject before he turned away. "I don't have time to fill out all these pages right now." "May I take the packet with me and return it tomorrow?" "I apologize for any inconvenience Mrs. Silva." "However, our employment intake packets are extremely confidential, and we do not allow any paperwork to leave our facility." "Thank you for your time," Brianna stated. "I will return tomorrow." She grabbed her hand bag which was an economical purchased she made four years ago from a consignment shop. After four years, it was extremely obvious that the bag was well used based on the tear in the handle and the unrecognizable faded decal on the face of the bag. Julius had by now lost interest and proceeded to walk down the hall. "Hello Dear," he stated as he picked up the phone. "Hey babe," the voice on the other end responded. "I am sorry to bother you at work, but I just wanted to call to see what you would like to eat for dinner tonight?" "You know I am not picky." "Whatever you put together is fine by me." "I wish just once when I ask that question you would respond with a real answer." "After 15 years I have such a hard time thinking of what to prepare." "I just want a little feedback babe." "The reason why I leave it up to you to decide my love, is because no matter what you make I will eat it." Preparing to lay it on thick, he added "I'll always eat what you cook because it's always good as long as you are the one who cooked it." Julius smirked as he rubbed on his man boobs and trailed his hands down to his stomach which was now a protruding 52 inches round. He knew he was quite the little charmer. Even after 15 years of marriage he still knew how to charm his wife into doing anything he wanted. Just as all the times in the past she responded; "ok babe, I'll see you when you get home." "Ok, I won't be late, so get ready for Big Daddy to make you remember why you married me." They both chuckled as Elisabeth responded; "ok babe, I love you." "I love you too;" as the phone clicked. Julius hung up the phone just in time. Upon placing the phone upon the receiver out rolled two farts in quick secessions which sounded like dog barks. "I am such a wonderful man;" he said as he stood up to fan away the stench. He grabbed his jacket and fanned the room a little more before putting it on. He looked at the clock on the wall. It was after 12:00 pm and the day was in full swing. "Carla!" He yelled from his office door. "Yes Mr. Kindle!" "Will you please come to my office with coffee, three creams, eight sugars, a note pad, and today's temp logs please?" "Yes sir," she responds. Julius sat at his desk with his head down engrossed in paperwork that had accumulated in a three-inch pile on his desk. Carla approached the door with coffee in hand knocked on the open door and entered. For a moment she thought she caught a whiff of smelly feet or rotten eggs. However, she dismissed the smell because it quickly went away. "Come in Carla, place the coffee on the desk, close the door behind you and have a seat please." "Is there something wrong Mr. Kindle?" "No Carla, door please." Just as she was told she placed the coffee on the end of the desk and walked away to close the door. When she turned around Julius was standing two inches away from her face. "Do you like your job Carla?" "Yes, I do she responded." "Mr. Kindle, I don't feel comfortable with you standing that close to my face." "Anyone could walk in here and see you standing in my personal space and assume the worst." "They will assume something is going on." "No darling, everyone knows that if my door is closed that means call first or they're getting fired." "That is just how things work around here." "Remember, I am the boss?" "What do you want from me Mr. Kindle?" "What every man wants sweetheart some apple pie and ice cream." "My wife is the apple pie and you can be my ice cream." He held up his hand and paused her from responding. "I love my wife, I just like to fool around a little." "Here is the deal if you taste good I will let you keep your job and maybe I will let you ride on my surfboard a few times." "What do you think about that?" At this point Carla was sure she was being pranked and she begin to laugh. Julius not being pleased by her reaction begin to give her a full body press with his lips gently planted on top of hers as he spoke. His breath smelled of coffee and the egg sandwich he had for breakfast. Carla was appalled from the stench of his breath and attempted with all her strength to push him away without dropping the papers she clinched in her hands. As he pressed his body a little harder against her she again attempted to forcefully push him away. "What are you thinking about at this very moment;" he asked? Trembling with unnerving energy as she responded; "Mr. Kindle I don't know what to think." "I am quite uncomfortable." He slowly lifted the hem of her knee-high skirt licked his index finger and placed it in the warmth of her wetness. "Don't speak; do you like your job here Carla?" "Yes sir, Mr. Kindle but not enough to be sexually violated." She begins to fight his advance and scream when he quickly cupped her mouth. "Hey, be quiet let me show you something." He slowly went a half inch higher reaching her g-spot and gave it 52 quick thrushes with his finger until the sounds of ocean waves formed. Before she knew it, she began to secret a watery substance down her leg and unto the floor. Before she was able to move or forbid him further he quickly retracted his finger. He placed his finger in his mouth and walked backwards to his desk and sat down. "*Hump!*" "*Woo hoo,* you taste like butterscotch!" "Now get out of my office and go to the restroom." You may wanna clean yourself up a little before you return to work." "10-4 good buddy;" he stated mocking her as he sat down and began viewing the files on his desk as if nothing had ever transpired. "Please close the door behind you on your way out." Nothing like that had ever happened to her before. Carla was in total disbelief. A part of her wanted to quit her job and scream at the top of her voice with disgust at the undeniable violation that had occurred. Deep inside she knew some part of her enjoyed what had happen. Carla had heard the office rumors regarding Julius and his chauvinistic ways, but she had never had an opportunity to personally experience what other women in the office described as his forcefulness, flattery and charismatic ways. He had always addressed her in a professional manner, right up until this point. Before this incident she felt almost invisible comparatively to the other women in the office. She quickly re-adjusted her skirt and turned the knob to leave with not so much as a glance over her shoulder to see if Julius was watching her. Walking quickly towards the restroom she notices the office gossiper looking over the cubicle wall directly in her path. She didn't have time for the tomfoolery; she needed to come to grips with the unnerving assault she just experienced. She quickly walked to the restroom. She pushed open the door and walked to the furthest stall which was the stall for women with physical disabilities. She lifted her skirt pulled down her panties and commenced to wipe dry all the wetness from her legs cleaning herself as best she could. When she exited the stall, she walked to the mirror and gazed at a reflection of her confused face. She sighed, "ah." "What just happened;" she wondered as she looked deeply into her eyes searching her soul for an answer that was evading her mind? "Shake it off," she said as she washed her hands and turn to the blower to dried them. She was in the middle of adjusting her form fitting skirt which nicely accented her size 8 frame and finishing her monolog when she heard the door open. In walks Thelma the office gossiper. "Are you ok Carla?" "Yes, I'm great; you?" "I am wonderful." "I just came in to check on you." "I noticed you looked a little flustered when you came out of Mr. Kindle's office just figured I would check on you and make sure everything was alright." "Like I said Thelma; I am fine!" "I just have a lot on my mind." "Alrighty then, I am here if you want to talk." "Thanks Thelma, I appreciate it, but I will be ok." Carla briskly walked out of the women's restroom to her desk. Thelma being the little greyhound that she was pushed open the doors of each stall and took a sniff as if to be completing a sniff test of DNA through the air. Carla sat down and began tapping on the keyboard of her computer waiting for the remaining 5 hours of the day to pass which she would then be at liberty to dismiss herself for a long restful weekend. She noticed Thelma walking pass her cubicle. As she glanced up Thelma pointed both her index and middle fingers towards her own eyes and then back out at Carla. This was a non-verbal way that people used to let others know that they were watching them. Carla was completely appalled. "What in blazing tarnations is wrong with these people," she thought? "I have got to be dreaming;" she said as she continued working. Carla was horrified. She was embarrassed, in disbelief and discombobulated by her experience. She didn't know what to do or how to react. She knew that in this day in time who would believe her? Who would take her seriously if she reported her account of events?

Elisabeth was just finishing up her day as she turned in her chair to look out the window as most of the staff was leaving the parking lot. She waved goodbye to Shelia and Caroline as they walked down the steps, into the parking lot, and departed to their vehicles. "Are you leaving Mrs. Kindle?" Elisabeth turned to see Mr. Walker the night building supervisor standing behind her. "Not yet Mr. Walker, maybe in another hour." "Yes, ma'am;" he responded as he walked to exit her office. "If I don't see you before you leave; have a blessed weekend." "Well thank you Mr. Walker, you too;" she responded as she stood up from her chair. Elisabeth was a very small woman with barely any definition to her frame. She was 5'5 with petite curves and 140 lbs; nothing like the women in her husband's office. She was always very quiet and reserved like she had a million things on her mind and most days she did. She was much of a mystery to many of her colleagues and most people who knew her. She was the epitome of a God-fearing woman; humble and meek. No one ever really knew when she was experiencing any type of tribulation. She was always upbeat with a smile on her face, a twinkle in her eyes and words of praise for anyone she spoke to on her lips. People enjoyed being around her because she always made them feel special or equal no matter what social or economic status they held. She addressed everyone the same. She treated everyone with the same respect, love, and tenderness. Even when people had wronged her she smiled and quickly forgave. Throughout her life she learned that she was not in control of the acts of other people. However, she could control the way that she reacted to them. Elisabeth sat at her desk reached inside her briefcase and retrieved her bible. She touched the outer cover, rubbing it as if it were a soft velvety blanket. She closed her eyes and prayed.

Lord, thank you for allowing me to make it through another day. If I don't make it home safe tonight, please protect my husband and children. Lord, I try every day to do your will in deed and in thought. Often, I fail but Lord, because of your grace and mercy I make it through the day and for this I say thank you. Lord, please continued to have mercy on every person that enters this building. Bless their families and every person associated with their name. Lord, please protect us all from the traps of the enemy. For every petition that is made to you whether in thought or openly submitted Father, please provide according to your will in Jesus name I pray Amen. She then opened the bible to her favorite verses of scripture Psalms 37 and proceeded to read the chapter in its entirety. When she finished reading the scripture she opened her briefcase just as before and gently placed her bible back into the silky fabric pocket. She had no clue the lives she touched by reading this scripture and praying every day before leaving work. Each day when she thought she was alone in her ritual to pray there were always three believers in the mist. Mr. Walker, Charlotte and Harmon. The fact was, they had all stumbled upon her praying one evening when they were about to enter her office to clean. They had learned about God and decided to give their lives to Him because of her and her prayers. She was unaware that she had changed the lives of three people because she prayed and allowed them to see the spirit of God in her. Mr. Walker, Charlotte, and Harmon the nightly Custodial Engineers learned of her ritual and began listening and praying with her each day over six months ago. Elisabeth was the nicest person they knew. They loved the fact that she had given them the name Custodial Engineers when she began working at Greenmast Production and Distribution Company 10 years ago. It made them feel appreciated and loved. They were not just the cleaning crew or janitors, but they had become her friends.

service announcement!" It was always surprising to him that this ritual continued to work for his entertainment. Nadine, the middle child was a 13-year-old eyeglass wearing, tall, mocha complexed, intelligent, fashionista who was in her first year of High school. She was erudite (well-educated) in cultural studies and spoke four languages. Her only interest when she was at home was reading old and outdated encyclopedias. The family home contained a library full of books. Their parents figured having a home library would be a great idea because some of the books they read growing up were no longer accessible in hard copies to children anywhere else due to the increasing development of technology. Elisabeth stood in the kitchen with barely a moment to breathe when in strolls Nadine. "Mom may I ask you a question of philosophical importance?" "Sure baby, sit let's talk." The family always had an open-mind and open-door discussion policy. So, no matter what was going on they had established that whenever any of the children wanted to talk about anything their parents would stop what they were doing to provide their full attention to them. "Mom do you think I am an astute (smart) and fledgling (inexperienced) individual?" "What?!" "Nadine why do you always have to use words that make me feel like I just walked onto the set of *What's Your IQ?*" Julius Jr comes walking through the kitchen and states; "mom what Nadine is asking is does she have a big head and small body?" "You know like a lolly pop." "Will you please stop teasing your sister?" "What is this about;" she asked? "You are a beautiful and bright young lady." "Why and what has you questioning your gifts from heaven?" "Nadine Shiloh La'Faris Kindle has a boyfriend!" "Julius, zip your face!" "I'm sorry mom, but she does, ask her!" "Well, Nadine what's going on?" "Mom, there is a young suitor who has come beckoning for my courtship but, he seems to think that my wealth of knowledge is somewhat intimidating." "What?!" "Mom, what she means is…" "Julius Gabriel Kindle Jr, if I have to tell you one more time!" Julius quickly grabbed his apple and bolted from the kitchen for he knew that a mention of his full legal name meant a sequel of pain was sure to follow. "Nadine, please tell me that you are not confused about who you are?" As Nadine looks down at her feet and begins to fidget. She clears her throat and states; "mother I never question who I am, but I do question whether my knowledge shall someday limit my chances of meeting a suitable spouse in the future." She looks her mother in the face and a shift in her mother's posture was ensuring that a lecture of truth was sure to follow. "Nadine, baby listen to me." Elisabeth stop in her train of thought for a moment. She knew she had to think about not chastising her daughter for having or wanting to have a boyfriend and think carefully of how to approach the subject. Otherwise, she knew Nadine would never talk openly to her again. So, she hesitantly stated; "any boy would be lucky no scratch that, he would be blessed to have a special person like you in his life." "You must love God first and then yourself." "Never question who God created when He made you." "If a young man loves God he will know how to love you regardless of your IQ." Nadine sat and pondered the encouraging words spoken by her mother. She then stood and turned to walk out of the kitchen but not before hugging her mother and thanking her for such insightful advice. After dinner Elisabeth looks up at the clock and noticed that it was late. She reached for her phone to call her husband and heard the jingling of keys in the door. "Hey baby! I know, I know, before you say anything I lost track of time and before I knew it eight O' clock had rolled upon me." "I am sorry," he stated. "So, I guess your phone wasn't working in the car on the way home either huh?" "Come on baby really?" "I don't want to have a tense moment with you right now." "I am tired and hungry." "I just want to eat dinner take a shower and hold my wife if that is ok with you?" As always, the humble, submissive and docile wife that Elisabeth was took control of her mouth. Elisabeth walked over to the stove and pile steamed vegetables, Red Russet potatoes, seared salmon with lemon and rosemary onto a plate. As she sat the plate in front of her husband she prayed over his food and leaned in to touch his shoulder. As she prayed; with her eyes closed Julius sat with a grin on his face shoveling small pieces of carrot, broccoli, and cauliflower in his mouth. When she closed her prayer with Amen he stopped chewing and mustard up the ability to say Amen in agreeance with his wife. She walked over to the refrigerator grabbed a cold bottle of water poured it into a clean glass and sat it in front of him on the table. She never said a word. In her heart and mind, she knew her husband was a cheat but because of her desire not to be hurt she told herself that this too shall pass. Even with all the proof she had; she would never allow him to know she was aware of his indiscretions. As she finished washing the dishes and walked towards the stairs she looked back at her husband who had been so engulfed in his text messages that he didn't have time to notice that she was watching him with a look of disappointment. She softly said; "I love you" and walked away. She walked up stairs to acknowledge the children and to tell them all good night. Then, went to the master bathroom to shower and prepare for bed. While in the shower she noticed the door slowly creeping open. She knew that only Julius would come into the bathroom when she was taking a shower. She also knew that he would soon be disrobing and infringing on her shower time that she used as prayer time with the Lord. As she braced herself for the ritualist neck kisses and explorative hand caresses; she tried not to think about which of his office staffers he had just left and explored in the same manner. She turned to look at him as he began to lather his body with soap and mentioned that her time in the shower was over. She thought that a quick step towards the towel rack would be his cue that she was not interested in his lustful self-satisfaction escapades. Oh, how wrong she was. He tightly grabbed her by the hand and said; "hey you are not done yet." "Come on baby not tonight she whispered." "Oh yeah, we are doing this." He continues, "beside I know what the bible tells you." He then begins to quote scripture. "*Ephesians 5:22-24 wives submit to your own husbands as to the Lord. For the husband is the head of the wife, as also Christ is head of the church; and He is the Savior of the body. Therefore, just as the church is subject to Christ, so let the wives be to their own husbands in everything!*" He looks at her with a death stare square in the eyes as if to dare her to challenge the Word of God. He brazenly states; "now am I right about it?" She knew without a doubt that he spoke the truth for he had memorized these verses of scripture from the beginning of their marriage for such occasions as this. As she hesitantly stands before him he goes on to state; "*1 Corinthians 7:4 The wife does not have authority over her own body, but the husband does.*" Then, he stops. She looks at him despondently; knowing very well the scripture that he cites has a second portion to which entitles the wife to the same right of authority over her husband's body. She wonders how then could he sleep with so many women if he loved her? She would not allow herself to verbalize what her mind was thinking for she knew that the task assigned to her hand was bigger than that of the present situation. He snatched her back into the shower and with the water running he pushed her down to her knees with a loud thud onto the shower floor. With his throbbing manhood in his hand he slapped her in the face and tells her to open her mouth. Being the dutiful wife, she complied. After 13 minutes of treating his wife like a street walker and violating every opening of her body he grabbed her by the neck and seal his disgusting violation of her body with a soft warm wet kiss to the forehead. He pushed her out of the shower and stated; "now you may leave." She looked into his eyes and wondered what she had done in life to have such disrespect and horrible treatment from the man who claimed he loved her. Julius smiled, winked his eye and said, "see you in bed for round two my love." Elisabeth slowly dried her body and silently prayed for God to save her. Julius then began to dance around in the shower like he had just conquered the world. Upon dressing and getting into bed Elisabeth prayed again to God and rolled over in bed and turned out the light. Julius emerged from the bathroom standing in the slither of light illuminating from the bathroom. He walked over to the bed dropped his bath towel and begin forcefully inserting his manhood into the darkness of her backside as if he was excavating a coal mine for buried diamonds. Even the muffled screams and cries from his fragile framed wife did not deter him from continuing until he climaxed. As she lay there shaking and crying from the painful experience he rolled over without so much as an apologetic kiss and fell asleep. Elisabeth prayed to God for protection of her body, for the sanity of her mind and for the comfort and peace of her broken heart. She always knew when her husband was cheating because he would often stay out later than normal and come home wanting to be intimate with her. He did this, so he could blame her if he contracted a sexually transmitted disease (STD). She lay in bed thinking about the time when they were younger and before the birth of her kids. Julius had slept with several other women and contracted an STD. He tried to blame her and stated that she was cheating. However, when they went to the doctor together it was founded that Julius was the only one of the two of them that had contracted an STD and

Elisabeth was clean. The doctor explained to Julius that it was impossible for her to have passed along an STD if she didn't have one. The doctor also explained that anytime a woman contracts an STD she may not know immediately however, her mate will. Symptoms typically arise in males quicker than in females depending on the type that has been transmitted. Elisabeth informed the doctor that she had not had sex with Julius in six days due to their busy work schedules and him never being at home. Julius dropped his head and then stated that he must have contracted the STD from a toilet seat which again was disproved by the doctor. Shaking the insulting memory from her mind Elisabeth quietly cried herself to sleep.

Brianna snatched on the doors of Kindle and Smith's Temp Agency only to discover the doors were locked. "Augh, I can never catch a break!" As she turned to walk away the locks on the door were released and a voice from behind her called; "What can I do for you Mrs. Silva?" "Oh, thank God;" she responded. "I was returning to fill out the application for the job." "It's Mr. Kindle, right?" "That would be correct," he stated and smiled. "Come on in let's get that packet started." "Matter of fact this is a better time because there are less distractions and I can interview you and decide right away." "You may be able to start on Monday." "Oh Wow!" "That would be great;" she stated! Brianna looked down at the packet some of the question seemed a bit personal, but she figured they were standard forms of questioning and didn't mind answering them because she needed a job like she needed air. Upon completing the 12-page employment intake packet which included an in-depth questionnaire about lifestyle preferences, marital status and willingness to work late, on weekends or alone with the boss. She walked to Mr. Kindle's office door, knocked and waited for his response. He opened the door and looked down at three specific questions and then responded; "you're hired!" With joy and excitement, she screamed; "yes, thank you, thank you so much Mr. kindle you won't be disappointed!" "I am a hard worker and I am never late or out due to illness." He smiled and muttered, "my kind of woman." "Excuse me," she stated? He replied, "I was just stating that you will be a great asset to the team." "When you come in on Monday I will set you up with Carla and she will teach you everything you need to know about the office and what is expected of you." "Thank you so much Mr. Kindle I really look forward to working with you and the company." "Don't you mean for me?" "No sir, I mean with you." "I am not a slave Mr. Kindle therefore the correct statement should be I look forward to working with you." "My you are beautiful and smart." "I appreciate the flattering comments, but again I am very married." "As am I," he stated. "Great, so we will not have any problems," she stated as she walked towards the door. "Oh um Mrs. Silva the dress code is formal, heels without stockings, dress or skirts no longer than two inches below the knee and white blouse if wearing a skirt." "We will have your name tag and scan key badge on Monday and this my dear will be your cubicle right here." He was pointing to an empty cubicle directly across from his office. "You may bring pictures, plants and anything you deem necessary to make it distinctively your own." "Thanks again Mr. Kindle I will be here by 7 am Monday morning." "No, make it 6 am," he stated. "Mr. Kindle, I thought you said that the office doesn't open until 8am and that all staff is required to be here by 7am." "Yes, I did." "However, with you being new to the office I need you to be here earlier so that we can get you settled before our temp laborers report for duty." "Yes sir," she stated.

As Elisabeth stood in the bedroom looking up at the ceiling she envisioned that she could see the Lord himself through it as she prayed. *Lord, it is I Elisabeth Renee Kindle, coming to You Oh Lord; first, to give thanks for all the blessings You have bestowed upon my family and me. Thank You for Your protection, love, mercy and grace. Father, I ask that anything unlike You in my life be removed so that I may be filled with Your spirit and do Your will.* Suddenly there was a knock at the door it was Julius Jr. "Mom, there is a man downstairs at the front door!" "Ok, I will be there in a minute." She pulls her hair up into a ponytail and walks downstairs to the door. "Hello, may I help you?" "Yes, I am looking for Mr. Kindle." "Is he home?" "No, but I am his wife." "How may I help you?" "I am sorry ma'am, but this is a matter that I am not at liberty to disgust with anyone other than him." "Ok, may I have your name so that I may informed him of who has inquired of him?" "Sure, my name is Scott Duval here is my card and contact information." "Please let him know I will be in touch." "Ok," she stated as she took another look at the card and watched as the strange man returned to his 2019 BMW. She noticed that he had a very distinctive tag with the word *Runner* on it and that he had travel from Wisconsin. "Mom who was that," Julius Jr. called? "I don't know some man here to see your father." Meanwhile back at the office Julius was searching online for women to deceive when the phone rang. "Hello dear," he stated. He knew it was Elisabeth because it was their home number on the caller ID. "Julius a strange man just left the house looking for you." "He left his card and said he will be in touch." "Did he say what he wanted?" "No, he said that he was not at liberty to discuss it with me." "According to the card his name is Scott Duval and according to his tag he is from Wisconsin." "What!" Elisabeth could almost feel the fear in Julius's voice as he yelled through the phone. "Are you in the kids ok?" "Yes, why?" "Julius, what is going on?" "Nothing baby, it's just weird that a strange guy all the way from Wisconsin would come by our house." "I just want to make sure you all are ok." "Yes, honey we are fine." "Just come home." "I don't understand why you insist on working on the weekend anyway." "No one else is working." "I know baby, but this is my company and because Mike lives over 1200 miles away he entrusts me to make sure our business and financial investment is running smoothly." "I will be home in a couple of hours." "Ok," she hangs up and prays to God to keep her family safe she has been with Julius for 15 years and she knows when he is lying; she feels in her heart that something is wrong. Julius sits back with his hands on his head and wonders. "How in the world did he find me;" he thought?" His train of thought was quickly broken by the ringing of his phone. "Hey baby," the soft seductive voice on the other end of the phone says. "Hey sexy, how are you," Julius responded? "I would be better if you would open the door and let me in." Julius walked to the back door of the building where he knew all his mistresses were trained to go when they wanted to meet up with him. The well-endowed woman gently kissed him on the lips and stepped inside. "How's my baby doing?" "I am well, I will be doing even better when I hatch our little man." "Hey, don't talk about my little quarterback like that," he said as he rubbed her stomach! "So, have you decided on the guest list?" "No, I thought you could help me when you fly back home, and we could sit down together and decide." "Ok baby, you know daddy got you." "So, what brings you here?" "Oh, I need another $2,000 to finish shopping for somethings for the baby's room and to pay the grounds keepers." "You should have just called and had me wire the money; why come all the way down here?" "I wanted to see you; is that ok?" "Yes of course, I'm sorry I just have a lot going on baby I didn't mean anything by it." "It's ok, I forgive you." "Besides I will use any excuse to come and spend time with my man." "Ok," he states; as he turned to work the combination to open the safe. He counted out twenty crisp $100 bills and stuffed them slowly into her bra. He reached in and grabbed her breast and slowly traced her nipple with his tongue. As she released a long soft sigh and whispered sweet nothings in his ear while biting the tip of his ear lope "I can't wait to be Mrs. Mike Smith." "Ok baby it will happen soon enough." "Now I need for you to go back to the house and get things squared away and I will be home in another two weeks." Julius thought he had it all figured out. Not only was he living a double life but the past that he once knew was about to catch up with him. If his wife knew that the man that she married was not Julius Kindle nor Mike Smith but a secret agent who faked his own death and got a face alteration she could have prayed for God to save them all from the ensuing pain that was sure to come. Julius had two wives, one fiancé and seven children between the three of them. He had been living a double life with Asia his fiancé for 2 years and on the run from Scott Duval and the mafia drug lords for 20 years. The presence of Scott aka The Terminator meant that his time here on earth was quickly running out. Julius stepped outside the door, turned to lock it and walk towards his car when the sound of two loud blasts rang his ears as he fell limp to the ground. His eyes grew dim and a grainy image of a tall thin woman and The Terminator appeared before him. As he struggled to breathe he could hear the woman say; "did you really have to shoot him like that?" Scott turned to Elisabeth and said; "for every time he forced himself on you and in you." "Yes, I did have to!" "He helped me raise your children Scott!" "Yeah well that is because he thought they were his!" "He didn't know that while he was out sleeping with other women, you were making love to me!" "Forget that jerk!" "He was just a job, or did you forget?" "Did you fall in love with him Lizzy?" "Did you?" "What!?" "No, you know I didn't!" "Well forget him!" "He wasn't a man he was a coward!" "So, like the coward he was he had to die!" "Wow!" "I hope you never feel that way about me or our children?" "You know I would never do that to my family." "The thought crossed my mind after you began sleeping with this man and living with him as your husband, but I realized you had to do what needed to be done to gain his trust." "20 years was a long time but to get this jerk it was all worth it." "Now please go and get Asia and tell her it is time to go!" "Tell her she can keep the $2,000 she just got from him as a bonus for the distraction she caused while the setup went down." Before he turned to walk away he gave one last look to Julius and kicked him in the stomach. Julius lay on the ground lifeless his eyes open and empty as they drove off down the alley. As soon as the car was out of view Julius slowly and quietly took small shallow breaths. He slowly reached into the holes where the two-gunshot blasts were to ensure that his vest was the only thing that had been penetrated. He began thanking God that The Terminator's aim was not at his face as he pulled off his bulletproof vest and fake blood bags which he wore every day to work. He stood unsteadily to his feet and placed everything into the dumpster. Reaching for his phone he pressed number eight on his speed dial. After the second ring the person on the other end picked up. "Hello?" "Hello, baby it's time." "Bring the bags and the passports it's all over." "Are you sure?" "yes, I am sure!" "It's all over baby; we will never have to worry about them again." "Ok, I will meet you at the spot." Julius quickly drove to the woods at the end of the city. There he parked his car and flung his keys over the cliff as he prepared to walk the two-mile hike into the woods on the other side of the city to his wife of 25 years. When he arrived at the edge of the woods he slowly and

The Life of Rose Dean

Rose Dean was born in 1944. A healthy baby girl. She came into the world with a confusingly pale complexion. Her grandmother quickly noted that she must hurry the child to her rightful complexion and decided that she must be left to the sun to acquire color and strength. For it was in those days that if you left a baby in the sun for most of the day the strength they would absorb from the vitamin D in the sun rays was astronomical. Rose Dean would not know until later in life of this story which would be repeated for her when she needed both physical and mental strength to overcome the obstacles of life.

Rose Dean was the only child born to the union of her parents Vera and Jefferson McMillan. Due to the fact she was an only child and struggled with the loneliness as she grew up. Rose Dean vowed to have as many children as the good Lord would allow when she became an adult. She was born in Gretna, Georgia just outside the Florida, Georgia border. She was the only child from her mother and father. However, her father was a rolling stone which gave her many half siblings outside of her two parents. She was the eldest of all her siblings and being the first born most of her family called her Jim which was her father's name. As she grew and began to become her own person; she realized she needed to be physically strong to protect herself from the glaring eyes of manish boys and men.

She walked, talked and lived as a Tomboy. Rose Dean grew up in the country and backwoods of Tallahassee, Gretna and Bainbridge, Georgia she learned that being an only child would bring much heartache. Her parents often worked to pay the bills and to provide for her. The work was hard and often took them away from home. When they went away for work Rose Dean would be left in the care of her aunt and uncle. She lived with her aunt and uncle for months while her parents worked and traveled for the sake of work.

Rose Dean lived with her aunt and uncle who were devoted Christians and believed in strict upbringing of children. There was church everyday and twice on Sundays. Sundays were often the best days because on Sunday afternoon each child would get an orange or an apple and 5¢ to do with as they pleased. Of course, they would all wait for ice cream truck to buy their favorite ice cream or pinwheel cookies. Regardless of their belief system and Godly connection Rose Dean felt as if she was often treated poorly by her aunt because she was not as feminine as her female cousins. She was often the one who had to lift her aunt's kangaroo pouch (fat belly overhang) to assist her with putting on her pantyhose before church. She also had to lift her into her wheel chair to help mobilize her for daily tasks. Even after she used all her strength doing these daunting tasks to assist her aunt she would then be sent out to work in the fields. Daily Rose Dean was sent to work in the fields alongside her boy cousins. She was forced to do hard labor with the same expectations as the boys. Rose Dean didn't mind the hard work however, she didn't want to be treated differently from all the other children. When she worked in the fields other males would taunt her about being a girl working in the fields because of her small thin frame. What they didn't know was that she had the strength of a grown man. Rose Dean learned to adjust to the life she was given and prayed for the time that her parents would no longer be absent from her life.

Rose Dean never understood why she wasn't allowed to do the things the other children could do. When she would ask her aunt and uncle about what she deemed as unfair treatment; her questions fell on deaf ears. There were times when her mother sent money home to her aunt so that Rose Dean would have money to purchase the things that she needed. She would be informed that the money had arrived, but she could not use it or ask for any. Her aunt had other plans and would keep the money locked away so that she was not able to use it for herself. One day Rose Dean watched her cousins going into the money stash which her mother had sent for her and decided that if they were able to use the money her mother had sent for her why wasn't she. She decided this would be the day her money would be used for her needs. She quietly walked over to the jar to retrieve the money she needed to purchase some items from the store. She was careful and noticed that there was a sudden calm about the room as she shelled out the quarters and dimes needed. When she turned around her aunt was standing there in the mist watching her take coins from the jar. With disappointment in her heart she dropped her head and prepared for the punishment that was sure to come. She was promptly punished for what her aunt stated was stealing from the jar. Rose Dean was a peculiar child growing up and she was very inquisitive. She enjoyed exploring the world and finding out about all the things life had to offer. She would often go into the woods to escape the glaring eyes of her aunt and uncle and the ridicule of her cousins. One day she ventured off and stubbled upon a kitten. This was her new-found friend and she vowed to love and care for it daily. She brought it home and fed it and quietly deemed it her own. She named it Tommy. After months of caring for it her aunt stumbled upon her with it playing and noticed that the cat was rather big. She forbade Rose Dean to have it and told her to send it back to the woods where she found it. Unknowingly to her Rose Dean was raising a wild cat or bobcat as they are known.

Rose Dean hated living with her aunt and her only escape was work and school. When she was in school she enjoyed being in an environment which allowed her the freedom to explore life with a new perspective, but she hated the way other students treated her. She felt the only way to gain their respect was to fight and establish how tough she was. This mindset not only made the other students afraid of her but also made them taunt her and treat her differently. She decided the only way to deal with the ostracism was to not speak. The teacher decided because of her inability to speak that she was uneducable and referred her to a school counselor for an evaluation. It was determined that Rose Dean's inability to talk at school had developed into selective mutism. The truth is Rose Dean was not a selective mute but was stubborn and chose to speak only when she felt the desire to. When in school she had performance anxiety and whenever she was given the task to speak or have class discussions she would shut down and refuse. During the 3rd grade she decided to enter in the school spelling bee. The other kids laughed and taunted for they all assumed that it was a joke. They knew Rose Dean refused to talk and engage during learning activities in class. How could it be possible that she would know any words let alone enough words to enter the school spelling bee. Oh, how wrong they were, and it wasn't until she won by spelling the words *compressed and liability* that they knew it. Rose Dean begin to enjoy school but as the turn of life would have it her mother became ill. Rose Dean decided to quit school and move to New York to live with her mother and grandmother. Being a young African American child during those days there were only two prominent jobs to have, one being a house maid the other a child care provider. She decided after working hard in the fields for so long that she would become a house maid. She tried to rely on her father for support with provisionary care of her mother and herself, but her father had other plans.

Her father decided he would travel with his friends singing in a quartet. Which left Rose Dean as the sole provider for her family. At the tender age of 14 she found work and thus began her life as a young woman with purpose in New York. After five years of cold weather and the need to provide for both an ill grandmother and mother she decided that the family should move back home to a place with warmer weather more conducive to her mother's health needs. The family decided to move to Bainbridge, Georgia and Rose Dean decided she wanted to return to school. Once enrolled she realized that what she had learned in 3rd grade the students were just learning in the 6th grade down south. She figured she already knew what they were learning and would return to school when she would be in a higher grade. Unfortunately, when she finally returned she had fallen so far behind in her schooling. She could no longer make adequate progress or gains to get back on track. Education was no longer an option in her mind and the need for an education wouldn't provide the necessary skills needed to provide for her family given their current and imperative state. She got a job cleaning homes and caring for the wealthy whites in town. At the tender age of 14 she met and fell in love with Frank the father of her first-born children. To their union were four babies Frank Jr, Earl, Verstine and a child that was still born. During those days health care was not as advanced as it is now, and the babies sometimes would get very sick and not live over the age of one. Rose Dean felt as if she was cursed.

She was losing her children to Sudden Infant Death Syndrome (SIDS). This devastated Rose Dean and she was slipping into a state of depression. However, her will was to remain focused and committed to work and provide for her family. This determination helped to stage away her feelings of hurt and depression. The deaths of the children took a toll on the young couple and they decided to part ways. After about a year Rose Dean decided that she needed to move on she met and fell in love with Willie. To the union of Willie and Rose Dean came a son who she named him Earth for he was her world her first surviving child. She was extremely excited and decided that she was going to do whatever it took to give him the world, so she worked extremely hard to be a great provider. His father Willie was a retired veteran who suffered from Post-Traumatic Stress Disorder (PTSD). Due to the death of her previous children she developed a habit of not sleeping. Every night she would get up and walk around the house several times checking to see if her child was still breathing and alive. To make matters worse her husband's PTSD began to become increasingly worse. She didn't know what to do. Often, she would wake up to sounds of shot gun blasts. Because of his PTSD he would have lapses in time when he would think that he was still in the war and would load his gun and shoot. His behaviors became so unpredictable and her love for him began to turn into pity and worry for her personal safety and the safety of their child. He would walk about the house daily carrying a loaded gun and tell her that people were out to kill him. He often forbade her to go to work. He told her if she opened the door the people who were after him would get inside and kill them. After having the heart stopping fear that he would hurt their son Rose Dean made a conscious decision to take their child and leave. She decided the safest place for her son would be to live with her mother. She worked hard and prepare to make a stable life for them. She worked and sent money home to her mother to provide for her son. Much to her denial she had begun to do to her child what she never desired. She had given him the same lifestyle she had growing up. She was leaving him with other relatives while she worked hard to provide the life that she desired for him. She worked hard and moved the family to a small town located in Mt. Pleasant, Florida.

During her time in Mt. Pleasant Florida she once again fell head over heels in love and met Richard. Once she settled in the small town of Mt. Pleasant, Florida. The life she lived was very different from her previous life with her previous relationship. She and Richard conceived a son and named him Isaac. She later conceived another child which she miscarried 4 months into her pregnancy. Richard treated her well. Every day he worked and brought home groceries to feed the family. At least that's what she thought until one day a neighborhood friend came by and told her that he didn't have a job. If she wanted to know what he was up to she should follow him one day and watch where he goes and what he does. Upon the advisement of this friend she followed him. What she witnessed was heart crushing and mind blowing. She witnessed him stand on the corner begging for money. When he was done he would go to the back of a supermarket where he had a friend steal and deliver food to him via the back entrance for a small portion of his daily collection. Upon his arrival home she questioned him regarding his daily activities and he lied blatantly to her face. Rose Dean made a declaration at that moment that she would never live a life dependent on a man to provide for her and her children.

Over the next few years Rose Dean conceived and bore more children. She moved her mother, her children and herself to Fort Myers, Florida where she had heard there were other members of her family living including her father. She met a man name named George and they had a daughter named Vera. The first girl child to live. She was ecstatic. Finally, she was having they family she always wanted. She continued to work, support her mother and live the life she always wanted. She got a job working on Fort Myers, Beach she cleaned homes for a wealthy woman and her husband who was very pleased with her work. They took to her so that whenever she had a need or want they willingly provided for her and her family just to keep her happy and working. Once she recalled that the woman paid a private dentist that she herself used for dental work. She paid him to remove all of Rose Dean's teeth and give her a beautiful set of porcelain veneer dentures to keep her from having to miss days of work due to tooth aches. She spent almost every year of her life since the age of 14 having children.

After life with George didn't seem to be working out as well as she would have like because he couldn't keep his desire to have other women out of their relationship she decided to move on. She then met the man who would be the father of her next five children. She met and fell in love with and married Leroy. To their union were six children Albertina, Ellendean and Jaellen Dean, Maranda, Tamika and one child unnamed of a stillborn birth. Leroy was a renegade man. He received joy from throwing parties, drinking alcohol and shooting his guns. Rose Dean had no idea the extend of his joy of fighting and causing incidents; she would soon find out. One night when they were out for a night on the town. They stopped into a night club to kick up their heels. Halfway through the night Leroy got into an altercation with another guy and his wife in the club which quickly escalated into a brawl. Leroy drew his weapon and unknowingly to him so did the other guy and they began to shoot at each other. Three minutes later both Rose Dean and Leroy sustained bullet wounds. She took two shots one to the head and another to the buttocks. She was quickly taken to the hospital where the doctors work expeditiously to save her life. Although, she had escaped death the doctor later explained that they were not able to remove the bullet from her head and that if they made such a risky attempt she would not survive the surgery. She had been given a war would for life. Leroy sustain minor nonlife threatening wounds and was arrested for the incident. He received a few years in prison for his involvement in the shooting.

Rose Dean decided that her life was not going to be that comparable to the wild west and after two years of reflecting on her marriage she filed for a divorce from Leroy. She then met Marion and they conceived a daughter. They named her Larouna. However, Marion was not a man who enjoyed sticking around. His motive for wanting to move around would never be discovered until his death over 21 years later. At the age of 35 Rose Dean's mother became terminally ill from complications due to diabetes which gave her another person dependent on her for primary care. It was approximately 5 months after the doctor's attempt to amputate her mother's foot that she finally passed away. Her mother stated and believe with all her being that she was taking all her body parts to heaven with her. She once stated that she would not let them cut anything off her body. She came into the world with all her body parts and that is the way she wanted to leave the world with all her body parts. Her mother soon passed away at the tender age of 49. Rose Dean went on to have more children. She had a daughter who lived 4 months and six days. She conceived again and had another baby girl that she named Rosemae. Rosemae's father was Randolph. She conceived Darren with Pelican, Rodney with Lewis and her last two children Brittany, one miscarriage and Lamille Jr. were all conceived by Lamille Sr. By the time she was 44 Rose Dean had bore 21 children. She continued to live life and attempted to provide the best life she possibly could.

Most men she dated were not up for the challenge of staying with a woman who had so many children and often her relationships with men never lasted long. She became a license contractor and worked with groups of farm workers, daily laborers and her eldest children. They would pick fruits, vegetables or whatever was in season. She owned three work vans and a station wagon which she used for transporting her workers and children. Rose Dean taught all her children strong work ethics before they reached the age of 14. By the age of five she had taught each of them how to collect eggs from chickens which she kept in the backyard. They knew how to wash dishes and clothes by hand in a foot tub with a wash board. Every weekend the family would load up in the car to go look for aluminum cans and cooper wire to supplement the family's income. Depending on how many cans they found they would come home and crush them one at a time with a cinder block. Most of the older children were also working part-time jobs to supplement the family income. Anyone over the age of eight would go to work in the field picking oranges, tomatoes, cucumbers or watermelons depending on the season. There were many days when the power would be shut off to the family home due to lack of income. Sometimes food would be limited. The children learned that syrup could be pour into water to make a beverage which closely resembled the taste of ice tea. Mayonnaise and bread, ketchup and bread and sugar and bread were considered sandwiches. The children learned to use oil/kerosene lamps and candles for light. They learned to boil water to take a bath by placing a big pot filled with water on an open fire pit they built in the back yard. Food would be prepared and cook outside on cinder blocks and an old refrigerator rack. They used dry tree branches for kindling. On some occasions the children were left to eat whatever was caught on the fish creek or capture from traps she set on her job in the fields. It was not uncommon to have wild hog, fish, turtle, coon, or deer on the menu for dinner.

There was always multiple people or groups of random children from the neighborhood at Rose Dean's residence. She worked multiple jobs which left the older children home raising the younger children and sometimes the younger children were left to raise themselves. Despite the perilous situation in which she faced she never received public assistance or welfare. She believed that because she helped to create her children; she would be totally responsible for them even if that meant with no help at all from their fathers to support them. At times, Rose Dean would become completely consumed by her situation and would leave for small vacations for a day or two and venture to her aunt's home just to sleep in peace without all the noise and distractions from her children running in and out of the house. By the time her eldest set of children were in their early teens they too were having children of their own making Rose Dean's situation more difficult. She not only had to provide for her own children but now she was responsible for providing shelter and food for her children and grandchildren. At one-point Rose Dean had 24 people living in her home including her children and grandchildren. There was never enough food, money, clothing, basic hygiene supplies or space. The children had to use baking soda for deodorant, tooth paste, to wash clothes and the dishes. Anything that required medical attention was resolved with leaves from trees in the backyard, Castro oil, orange and grapefruit peels, onions, Vicks vapor rub, Vaseline, cobwebs, benadine, or a shot of vodka. The rooms in the home were filled to max capacity and there were always multiple fights among the children. At one-point Rose Dean came home to three of her daughters in the backyard fighting with knives and razors; two of them were bleeding. There was just too much chaos and not enough order. To ease the stress of having 24 people in a five-bedroom home she decided to move out of the family home into and apartment down the street and allow her children to have her home and take care of themselves. She only took the youngest three children. After multiple incidents involving the police and bad company at her home she came back about two years later and ask that everyone ages 14 years and older to move out. She had done all that she could do and had given all that she could give to assist them in becoming productive adults and she had enough. Although, at the time the children didn't quite understand the reason or the level of stress she had that influence their mother's decision to put them out. They respected it and later grew up and became stronger, smarter and more self-sufficient than anyone would have ever imagined. As the years passed Rose Dean lived a life of struggle, tireless hours on jobs that pay less than $15,000 a year and gave her all to continue to provide for her family. Throughout her life she has endure being shot in the head, being struck by lightning and in a car accident that would have taken her life if not by the grace of God. She nearly lost her home in a house fire set by a girl who lived in the neighborhood who was upset with one of her children. She pulled through a stroke and a minor heart attack. She has buried nine of her own children two grandchildren and one great-grandchild. She has outlived all but two of her children's fathers. Rose Dean is an amazingly strong woman. She worked hard for everything, lived off the land, never depended on a man or the federal government to help financially provide for her children. Most importantly Rose Dean created a family dynasty through the birth of her 21 children. Rose Dean still lives in Florida with her current husband of 20 years. She has children living in New York, Virginia, Mississippi and Florida. When asked her greatest accomplishment she stated; "my greatest accomplishment was having my children and being alive long enough to see you all grow up."

The Force of Life's Confessions

"Hey Stephanie, wait up girl!" "Dang you walk fast." Stephanie was on a mission, she had to meet Roger before he went to class. Roger was a worry wart and he would have a panic attack whenever she was late. "Hey Step, are we still on for tonight," Kim asked? "Oh yeah for sure," says Stephanie. "Alright girl, I will catch you later," said Kim as they parted. Stephanie was going to borrow her mother's car, so they could all go and hang out on their last night as high school juniors.

It was the end of the school year and they were all setting out to make waves in their very small yet, tight knit circle of friends for the upcoming year as seniors. Stephanie, Naomi, Lucy who they called La La, Mia, and Kim had all been friends since grammar school. They had spent of their lives together and they were more like sisters then friends. Later that evening they made plans to drive around the west side of Delray City. While riding around in Stephanie mother's two toned 1984 Ford station wagon the girls prepared themselves to make their rounds in the local neighborhood projects. Although their means of transportation wasn't anything to sneeze at it was all they needed to experience the will to be free from the glaring eyes of their parents on the weekend. Stephanie mother's car was huge, with enough room for the entire girls' basketball team. The car was covered in dark grey primer with what was left of its original hot pink paint job. The car had two thick white wall tires on the front and two oversized tires on the back. Every time the car hit a pot hole or bump it would bounce high enough to give the girls that queasy feeling in the pit of their stomach; like the feeling they would get from the rides at the county fair. Stephanie's mother always kept her crushed aluminum cans in the rear of the car. The girls would often tease Stephanie about her mother's eccentric hobby. Stephanie would always defend her mother's right to collect aluminum cans by stating; "my mother is doing her part to help preserve the earth through recycling." Stephanie's mother also had a very distasteful set of pink and black dice hanging from the mirror. Despite Mrs. Strom's poor designer taste for her car, she was very eloquent, classy and had great fashion sense when it came to all her other material possessions. Her station wagon was one of four family owned cars which she seldom used. The car had been in the family for over twenty years. Mrs. Strom considered it to be a family heirloom since it was the last of her father's material possession in which she owned after he passed away sixteen years ago. During their weekend excursion the girls were all dressed to impress. The girls took pride in their ability to dress in the latest fashions'. While planning and plotting earlier that evening they had foreseen a future of finding an interesting hangout to acquire social stimulating conversations about the next year's popularity contest. The girl's weekend ritual consisted of them all chipping in for gas and food. They had devised this plan because it was a lot cheaper and it allowed them to have money available for the next weekend's excursion just in case their parents felt the need to deduct from their allowance due to some unforeseen error they would make such as over extending themselves at the mall. Although the girls were social bunnies they were economically gifted. As they listened to Luther Vandross's Here and Now on the radio they fixed their makeup, hair and were ready to hit the scene. They wanted to make sure they were well put together before driving through the West Side Projects. As they drove up to the light on 47th and Manny Terrace they could see the lights on the courts. Stephanie pulled up to the courts and parked. There was always a gang of college guys playing basketball on the courts because it was so close to Delray University. Stephanie, Lucy and Naomi were the first to exit the car. The girls begin gossiping while looking at the guys and laughing loud enough to get their attention as they exited the car. They sat on the top of the car and watched as the guys who were much older and sophisticated shoot hoops. As Kim and Mia joined the other girls they all pretended to be too engrossed in their own conversation to notice when the guys stopped briefly to gawk at them. Stephanie was the only one of the girls who truly ignored the guy's advances for she was Roger's girl. Roger and Stephanie had been together since middle school and they were as she loves to coin as her own personal phrase laying and staying together for life. As Kim stood watching Stephanie blow kisses to Roger through the fence she pondered how she could never really understood how Stephanie was willing to sacrifice her future and her soul by giving up her precious temple to Roger so frequently. After discussing all the drama that happen in school the girls decided to walk closer to the courts and sit on the bleachers. As they all walked along the fence on their way to the bleachers they played their ritual of cat and mouse with the guys. They would yell through the fence talking to the guys and then when the guys eagerly responded to their playful advances the girls would then pretend not to hear them. They would look at the guys just long enough to let them know they were interested; as soon as the guys responded or made advances to this behavior they would turn away. As they walked along the fence Kim began to ponder the lives of her friends and her very own. Stephanie although she was proclaimed by Roger received the most attention whenever the girls went out. She was 5'9 145 lbs. with a 24-inch waistline and hips that were the size of Christmas hams. She was the daughter Mr. and Mrs. Strom a.k.a Mr. and Mrs. Neighborhood Watch. Stephanie was very strong minded, determined and the leader in the group. She seemed to be the only one of them who was truly ready for all that the world had to offer. Then there's Lucy with a statue of 5'6 160 lbs. and an apple bottom that she got from her mama. She had the shoulders of a quarterback and the hands of a pianist. She was the daughter of Mr. and Mrs. Dr. Ted Fugal. Her mother was biracial mixed with Chinese and black which in turn gave Lucy her beautiful bronze skin tone free from blemish and silky hair that ran down her back. Although she was built and stack in all the right places, she would not allow her physique to be misinterpreted as a young woman whose size and shape was over compensating for lack of knowledge. This susta had a GPA of 4.06 and wasn't afraid to flaunt it with her use of elaborate words in conversation. Unknown to others Lucy embarked upon the opportunities to discuss politics with some of the most educated school staff and their affiliates just because she was bored. Then there are Naomi and Mia identical twins they were the real fun of the group they were both 5'4 125 lbs. with hazel eyes and sandy brown hair. They were very petite right down to their size 5 shoes. Their ability to be comical was phenomenal. They were always telling jokes and making everyone laugh. They made jokes about everything right down to their size. They chuckled and talked about their ability to dine at any restaurant in town for the price of 12-year old. Although their friends would all laugh when they told these jokes they knew it was their way of dealing with their very petite sizes. They were the second set of twins born to Mr.

and Mrs. McNapple. Their friends always stated that they could only imagine what Mrs. McNapple must have thought after being pregnant for the second time to find out she once again carried twins. Then there was Kim standing 5'8 150 lbs. golden brown skin, brown eyes and shoulder length black hair with sandy brown highlights. She had an ideal build; all her measurements ending in even numbers 36, 24, 36 she was the advisor of the group. Her parents, Mr. and Mrs. McMillan were both in the field of education which translated to her as be the professional advisor of her group of friends. Kim honestly thought this was her purpose, to give advice to all those who would and wouldn't listen. As they all sat down on the bleachers Kim gave her friends a smile which must have indicated she had been off in her own little world. As soon as Kim smiled her friends mention to her the fact which she must have not been listening to a word which was said because the response was not that which was warranted. As Kim quickly responded with, "huh?" "Never mind," Stephanie said; as they all sat watching the game until it was over. The game ended at 10:30 pm the guys wrap it up because they knew the lights on the courts shut off promptly at 10:45 pm. After the game Stephanie ran over to Roger and they begin doing that annoying thing they do, rubbing heads together and kissing. Stephanie always knew how to stroke Roger's ego by telling him he was the star of the game. Everyone else knew better they knew the reality; that in fact Roger's game sucked. It was only the influence of his older brother Fredrick that prompted the guys to even let him on the courts to play with them. After the game Roger introduced the girls to his brother and his college friends who had up until this point had been just a bunch of cute guys gawking at them. There was Mike who was 6'1 build like a black version of Batista. Then there is Chauncey who was 6'3 who was built like David Justice that fine professional baseball player, next there was Phillip who was 6'0, slim, trim in all the right places with a pack of abs so tight they look like a brand new wash board, Fredrick Roger's older brother was 6'2 mysteriously handsome with his slanted green eyes, butter cream smooth, glistening caramel colored skin and biceps the size of tree trunks and of course there was Roger. Although Roger favored his brother they did not have the same build, Roger was a bit on the puny side. The guys all stood around allowing hormones and the curiosities of the opposite sex take control over their creative young minds. Meanwhile the girls laughed about how many shots Roger missed during the game. They all talked for about 10 minutes until which the lights on the courts clicked off. Then Mike suggested they all continue their conversations at Mildred's Soul Food restaurant. The girls agreed and followed the guys in Phillip's tricked out 1990 Cutlass.

They all arrived at Mildred's restaurant a little after 11:00 pm. The girls pulled into the parking lot very slow. They could see the guys passing around a small canister of breath spray and the girls watched as they wiped the sweat off their glistening bodies. After arriving to a neighboring parking spot, the girls exited the car slow and gracefully as if they were top models being called out on stage one by one. Stephanie of course wasting no time jumped out of the car and ran over to Roger she grabbed his hand saying "let's go." The girls knew why Stephanie liked being the first to sit. She would always want to sit facing the window for what she called the perfect view. Stephanie also liked to sit on the inside of the booth she always had some strange explanations for her compulsive behavior which never made sense to anyone but her. The rest of the guys and girls stood outside for 2 minutes trying to choose up their honorary dates for the night. The girls decided they would sit next to the guy that they felt was attractive enough to occupy their time for the next hour or so. Kim just wanted to sit next to the guy she felt was the least likely to hit on her. Of course, she would pretend to be interested when he indulged her with the most boring conversation. Nevertheless, it was one night and unless things went undoubtedly well between the guy she chooses she wouldn't have to worry about seeing him again. Lucy and Phillip hit it off ever so quickly it seemed as if they had known each other for years and they had so much in common. The young inquisitive apprentices all sat around discussing hobbies, careers, life, likes and dislike as Charlotte the waitress walks over to take their orders. "May I start y'all off with something to drink?" Phillip responded with "yes ma'am ah let us get a couple pitchers of beer please." It was at that moment Kim began to realize that they were practically on dates with older men. She had never actually been on a date let alone with anyone older. She looked at the others who seemed to be too busy having a conversation to notice what had happened. Clearing her throat, she said; "excuse me they don't speak for me and may I have a sweet tea with a slice of lemon please?" Charlotte nodded her head in acknowledgement. "Is there anyone else who would like something else to drink?" The other girls followed Kim's lead, "yes ma'am sweet teas for us also," they responded, and Charlotte quickly walked away. Then Kim coughed twice and excused herself from the table looking at the girls as they related to the signal for them to excuse themselves. When the girls arrived at the restroom they all begin talking at such a rate that neither of them could understand the other. After about 15 seconds of this they all begin to laugh, and Kim mentioned that no one seemed to notice when Phillip ordered beer for the entire table. Upon mentioning this they didn't seem to care yet, Kim was very concerned. She knew that they all had at least one parent who consumed one or more alcoholic beverages a day. Therefore, she was aware of the unconscious statements that would come out of the mouths of those who were slightly delusional from the intoxicating drink of choice. Naomi and the others begin to laugh and talk about what they thought of the guys. Stephanie wasn't amused by their little school girl crushes and proceed to return to the booth. The rest of them stood there talking about what they would say and do if these guys consumed a little too much to drink and things got a little uncomfortable. They decided that if things were to get a little too hot to handle they would all make up an excuse to leave, putting the pressure of Stephanie to take them all home therefore she would be over ruled if Roger tried talking her into staying just a little while longer. As they walked back to the table the guys were so engulfed in conversation they had barely noticed when the girls returned. To the girls' surprise when their appearance became apparent to the boys they all stood up like perfect gentlemen and allowed them to sit before returning to their conversation. Charlotte the waitress walks over when the girls return to take their orders. Everyone sort of took to the person on their left as they were getting to know each other a little better. After eating they had all decided it was time to end the night. The guys had to go back to their dorms to prepare for a long day of training tomorrow. They were all on the same athletic scholarship which required them to have curfews, steer clear of agents, and not to enter coercion through gift acceptance. "If you guys are so keen on following the rules with curfew and whatnot why on earth would you all sit up the night before a long day of training and drink alcohol;" Kim asked? "Well excuse us coach, yet we thought since we are already restricted from everything else we would at least have a drink or two so as not to be completely cut off from the world." The guys all don't let ya'll ages start making ya'll smell your musk." This was something all the elders said when they felt as if a child was acting a little too mature before their time. Then to their surprise she stopped scolding them and sent everyone to bed, but halting Kim for a brief minute. She asked her; "Kim how you are doing baby?" She could sense something was wrong because this was very unusual. Then she responded; "is there something wrong?" Mrs. Strom then burst into tears weeping and unable to talk. Kim didn't know what was about to happen, but she knew it wasn't good. Mr. Strom put his hand on her shoulder and said; "Kim, have a seat baby we've got something to tell you." Kim didn't remember when she hit the floor and had no knowledge that she had fallen but moments after hearing the news it seemed as if she was dreaming and that she would wake up at any moment. After asking them what happen and how did she get down on the floor she heard the words that she would remember for the rest of her life. "Kim your father was killed today in a 10-car pileup on the interstate near Nocatee." "Your mother has gone to Nocatee County morgue to identify the body." They continue talking and telling her everything they knew regarding the accident and the information which had been conveyed to them. Kim's body had gone completely numb. She could no longer hear anything. She knew everyone was talking because by this time she could see all her friends had rejoined her and Stephanie's parents in the living room attempting to console her. Kim didn't remember much those 7 hours before her mother return from Nocatee. Kim did however, remember the devastating look her mother had on her face the day she arrived to pick her up. Her mother had huge bags under her eyes; her hair was completely a mess. She had the appearance of a woman who had been working out all day and forgot to shower. In those 7 hours her mother looked as if she had lost 20 lbs. With tear filled eyes Kim met her mother half way across the Strom's front yard with her arms out like a three-year-old waiting to be picked up. At that moment her mother's hug felt like the comfort of one of those warm blankets they give you out of the heater in the hospital. They must had been standing in the middle of the yard crying for about 10 minutes before Mrs. Strom came out and invited them in for some lunch. Mrs. Strom and Kim's mother begin to hug and cry. Mrs. McMillan and Mrs. Strom had been friends since middle school much like Stephanie and Kim the two of them were very close. Kim knew her father was gone, and she would never hear his voice or see his smiling face again yet, the presence of her mother made her feel as if everything was alright.

After they devoured their lunch Mrs. McMillan took a shower as both she and Kim prepared to head home. Although the drive from the Strom's residence to the McMillan home wasn't very far approximately 35 miles total distance it seemed to take forever to get there. As they traveled home Kim began to question her mother about her father's accident. Kim knew it was hard for her mother to deal with these questions so soon yet, the desire to know what happen overwhelmed her even more. Kim wanted to know how the accident happened and was it her father's fault. The anticipation of knowing the truth was tearing her apart she wanted to know was it his fault or the fault of some careless person with total disregard for her father's life. Mrs. McMillan explained the accident as the investigating officer told her. She said that Mr. McMillan had been caught in the middle of the 10-car pileup and from his investigation he had no knowledge of what happen to him for he was hit with such an impact of force that he had died instantly. He was traveling in the northbound lane when a car jumped the median hitting a truck carrying hazardous chemicals causing it to flip over which begin the inevitable pile up that stole her father's life. Kim then asked the devastating question "Mom do you think daddy knows he's dead?" "Kimberly Elisha McMillan shut up!" Kim knew the moment those words flew out of her mouth that they were just the words her mother needed to push her over the edge. She'd apologized a million times and ever so quickly, but the damage was already done her mother begin to cry so hard her shoulders begin to shake uncontrollably as if she was going into insulin shock. Kim talked her mother into pulling over and she wrapped her arms around her. The two of them sat parked on the side of the freeway trying to comfort and console one another. Mrs. McMillan explained to Kim that her father had talk to her just last week about retiring. She was trying to convince him that he was still in the prime of his life and too young to retire. Kim explained to her mother that her father being on the road at that time was not her fault and that even if she had not expressed her desire for him to continue working it didn't mean he wasn't going to continue to work anyway. No matter how they tried to rationale their thoughts of her father's death they both knew that he wasn't coming back. After they regrouped and mentally pulled themselves together her mother pulled back on to the freeway and they continue heading for home. As they pulled into the drive way she heard her mother breathe in very deep and release a huge sigh as if to say; this house is no longer a home because her father wouldn't be there. She turned off the car and took the keys out if the ignition. Her mother just sat there and stared at the front door. "Ma come on." Her mother just sat there, Kim shook her shoulder "ma come on we got to deal with this sometime." Kim truly knew the reality was that they couldn't stay outside in the car forever. As they walk towards the door it felt as if they were both taking steps to the end of a cliff and getting ready to jump to their deaths. Kim unlocked the manner of dialect. Kim's aunt walked over and kissed her on the cheek with bacon grease around her mouth. "I can't stay small forever" Kim says, with a half-smile placed on her face to cover the pain in her heart. Although she was pleased to see her aunt and uncles they only reminded her of her father's death. "Hey niece tell me something you still writing that der poetry stuff you be writing?" "Yes sir, Uncle Danny." "Good," he says; "one day you going to make your mama rich." "You going to show me some of them before I leave?" "Yes sir," Uncle Danny." "I didn't know you write poetry" her aunt Sasha said. "I don't talk about it much because it's just something I do for fun." "I'd love to hear some of it too if you don't mind." "Yes ma'am" Kim said, as she heard the door bell ring. She walked to the door and there stood Stephanie, Roger and Fredrick they had all drove over to check on Kim and her mother. Although, Kim mentioned a phone call would have been fine she was ever so pleased to see her best friend standing in the door way. She invited them in and introduced them to her uncles and aunt. Her mother invited them in for breakfast as they walked toward the kitchen. Fredrick said; "much obliged ma'am," Kim said, "much a who?" Then she heard her uncle laughing. As he said; "boy you must have been raise round some old folks." "Yes sir," Fredrick responded. He explained that his grandparents raised them when their parents went overseas to study ancient Egyptian Artifacts 7 years ago. Kim thought to herself, it was very comforting to have people around during this very depressing time in their lives. They all talked and laughed about the good times in their lives and the way her father would always be the life of every gathering. They all made references by way of stating, if he was here now what he would say. After breakfast Kim and her friends begin to clear the table and wash the dishes to make it a little easier for her mother. Kim's uncles and aunt talked her mother into getting dressed and going out for the day to face one of her fears. Kim's mother had to shop for her father a suit for his burial. Kim's uncles and aunt had to assist in the difficult process as well as making the final decision for the funeral. Despite Kim's efforts to just stay at home her friends seemed to be the honorary persuasion coaches for doing the same for her getting her out of the house and getting her mind off the horrific, traumatic heartbreaking pain of the sudden death of her father. After Stephanie convinced Kim to get dressed they all sat talking to her family about their afternoon plans and discussed meeting back at the house for dinner at a feasible hour. Stephanie, Roger, and Fredrick were all very comforting. They drove over to the North Port Mall to shop for a dress for Kim to wear for her father's funeral. Of course, Stephanie was the shopping guru therefore anything that Kim decided to purchase would have to have her stamp of approval at least she thought so. The girls ventured into Dress for Success to look for the perfect dress as the guys stood quietly and patiently waiting. It wasn't until that moment that Kim decided to ask Stephanie out of curiosity; "Why in the world is Fredrick with y'all," she replied? "He heard about your father's death when Roger was talking to me over the phone and he wanted to make sure you were O.K." Although, Kim was very shocked at his compassion she was also moved. After forty minutes Kim found what she considered to be the perfect dress it was a very silky and sleek black and white spaghetti strap Versace that hugged her body and accentuated her curves with a matching jacket. Kim put on the dress and stood in the mirror. Although, the dress was beautiful she thought about the reason she was buying the dress in the first place. As she stood staring at herself she reflected to the day her father took her to the mall to by her first prom dress for the junior high school dance and how he didn't want her to go he took her to buy the dress anyway just to see the smile on her face. Kim then had a black out and the next thing she knew she was sitting in a chair as one of the store clerks was handing Stephanie a cup of water as Fredrick and Roger fanned her. "Would you like for me to call the paramedics;" said the clerk. "No thanks, she will be fine," Stephanie said. "Kim, hey girl are you ok?" Kim responded by nodding her head and asking Stephanie to promise she wouldn't mention any of this to her mother. Kim didn't want her mother to worry about her. Kim then proceed to pay for her dress and bought matching shoes before deciding to call it a day and head for home. On the way Kim could hear Roger and Stephanie discussing Stephanie staying with her. Meanwhile, Fredrick and Roger would return home as they agreed. The four of them headed for Kim's house. When they arrived Kim's, mother was still out, and Stephanie said that she was going to drive the boys' home. Kim gave them all hugs and a kiss as she said goodbye. "I'll come back later with the girls;" Stephanie said. Kim shook her head to acknowledge that she heard Stephanie and walked into the house. As Kim sat alone on the living room on the couch she turned on the T.V waiting for her mother, aunt and uncles to return. She realized this was the first time she had been alone in the house since her father was killed. She walked up to her mother's room door and slowly pushed the door open. She didn't know what she expected to see but a part of her wanted to see her father sitting on the edge of the bed taking off his shoes after work like he always did. She saw the picture of her father that her mother had been holding the night prior. She walked over and picked it up. She looked at the picture in stared in her father's eyes and at that moment she thought she heard a voice say in a soft whisper "I will always be right here." "Oh no," she said. "I am not going down that road." "I know you are dead in there is no way I am going to even pretend that I heard that!" She placed the picture back onto the night stand, close the door and went to her room. She closed the door and pulled out her poetry note book and begin to review all the poems she had written. She began reading them one by one until she heard a knock at the door. "Who is it?" She didn't hear anyone respond so again she said, "Who is it?" No one responded so she got up and walked over to the door. She opened the door, and no one was there. So, she shut the door back and lie down on her bed staring at the pages in her notebook again she heard a knock. "Ok somebody has jokes." "If I come out swinging you'll stop playing, won't you?" Then again there was no response. Picking up the phone she called Stephanie. The phone rang twice, and she heard; "what's up, you Ok?" Kim spoke with terror in her voice because when she said; "No." Stephanie paused and said, "Ok I'm on my way." Kim thought to herself Stephanie must have stop at the store on her way before leaving or she had broken several laws getting to her house because in a matter of four in a half minutes she was knocking on the door. "Kim!" "Kim!" "It's Stephanie open up the door!" "*Sssh* be quiet," Kim said. "I think someone is in my house." Stephanie signal for Roger and Fredrick to come quick. "Did you call the police?" "No, because I don't know if anyone is actually hear." "If I call the police and I don't know if anyone is in here they are going to think I am crazy." "That don't make sense Nee Nee." Kim only called Stephanie Nee Nee when she was worried because Stephanie's middle name is Denise. Kim explain to them what happen with the door and Stephanie stated that maybe it was someone outside in the neighbor's yard which made sense. Although, she explained it sounded as if they were knocking on her room door. Stephanie then stated that they would stay with Kim until her mother, aunt, and uncles arrived just in case she heard the noise again this way she would have witnesses. Around 5 o'clock that evening Kim's mother, aunt, and uncles arrived with loaded arms. Kim and her friends all pitched in to help bring in things from the car and put them away. Kim gave Stephanie a look out the corner of her eye as to say please don't say a word about today when her mother asked how their day went. Mrs. McMillan freely admitted being tired she slowly sashayed to the kitchen and prepared to cook dinner. Despite her physical and mental state of being Mrs. McMillan mustarded up the strength to entertain Kim and her friends by way of asking them how their day went Stephanie stated, "after Kim found a dress we all just decided to hang out here." Kim's mother was pleased to hear her friends were so supportive. Mrs. McMillan then invited Stephanie and the guys to stay for dinner. Stephanie stated, "Mrs. McMillan it's getting late and I have got to get the guys home." After further assertion of Mrs. McMillan's decisive negotiating for them to stay Stephanie agreed. "I need to call my parents to get permission." "I will call everyone's parents and get permission so there is it settled you all will stay, and I don't want to hear another word about it." After dinner everyone sat around talking and their conversations ran late into the night. Kim's mother loved all the company. Kim thought it was her mother's way of having an excuse to not to deal with the loneliness she felt from not having Kim's father around. She had advised Stephanie, Roger and Fredrick to stay over because the drive during this time of night would be too dangerous. Kim's aunt and uncles prepared to leave to go back to their hotel. They all shared hugs, kisses and handshakes said goodbye and goodnight. Mrs. McMillan proceeded to call the Strom's and Addison's to receive their approval for an overnight stay of Stephanie and the guys before heading off to bed. Kim pulled out the extra blankets and provided a demonstration of how to open the let-out couch and cots for the guys. She quickly

Night to Day

Desperate, paralyzing screams for attention.
Looking beyond a horizon of guilt free hope fails to mention.
A souvenir from a memorable vacation leads to compassion; for
the wilted mind of a confused insane man with no passion.
Passive aggressiveness as frustrated tempers express
themselves during a nurturing time for God to bless.
This is a time for night to turn into day.
Children rob a store just to fill their stomachs of hunger
which ends in a battle for a resting place six feet under.
A mother screams for sorrow and a wish to turn back the
hands of time; with the pleads of a bargaining chip she would
give her last dime. This is a time for night to turn to day.
A father with all hope lost and a last chance over shadowed
by the color of his skin decides to shorten his
struggle. He uses one blast of steel to his central nervous
system. This is a time for night to turn into day.

Just when she was about to push open the door to comfort
her mother she felt a hand on her shoulder. Kim turned around
and there was Fredrick standing there with one finger over his
lips giving her the sign to be quiet. He whispered in Kim's ear;
"your mother has been up for at least 3 hours crying and talking
to your father's picture." "It's best not to bother because this is
her way of healing." As he pointed, and they quietly went to
the kitchen Kim asked Fredrick, "How do you know this?" He
explained to her that this was his course of study. He said he
was learning about Psychology in college and upon graduation
he was going to be a psychiatrist. When Kim first met Fredrick,
she thought he was all muscles and no brains but the more she
talked with him she soon discovered that he was a cool guy.

As they sat talking and sometimes pausing just to share simple and quiet moments enjoying each other's company Kim and Fredrick begin learning more about each other than even their closest friends knew about either of them. Kim stood up quietly with a glazy sparkle in her eye and offered Fredrick some cake and sweet refreshing orange juice to wash it down. He gladly accepted. As they sat drinking juice and nestling every morsel of delectable moist orange pound cake they decided it was time to head off to bed. Kim suggested she was going to have a look in on her mother who by this time had fallen asleep with the picture of her father in her arms. Kim thanked Fredrick for his very intellectual conversation and headed off to bed. Kim didn't know what it was about the conversation she had with Fredrick yet, she couldn't stop thinking about him. Eventually she too dosed off only to wake up hours later with Stephanie trying to lift her eye lids asking was she going to stay in bed all day. Kim gently opens her eyes as she recites: "It's always a pleasure to be seen as a need you reach out for a goal and beyond a wholesome plead." "Walking on a beaten foot path just to see a beautiful image of an envisioned course of action that everyone has seen." "Waiting for a wonder to fill an empty mind while whistling a song of mischief that has crossed a frozen heart with revenge that is benign." "A shadow pattern reflects a lesson which fails. Watching the waters of the river cast off a familiar smell." Stephanie responded with a dazed look; "What?" "Gurl get up!" By the smells coming from the kitchen Kim knew that was going to be impossible to stay in bed she could smell the scents of blueberry waffles, hot crispy bacon and scrambled eggs. "*Mmm* mama's cooking breakfast"; she said as she rolled out of bed. "Hey!" "What happen between you and Fredrick last night nasty?" Stephanie always seemed to have a life-long habit of asking questions that made people just want to respond ever so quickly the way she worded this seem to make even the strongest of her accompanist respond defensively. "What?" "Huh?" "Nothing happened," said Kim. "Girl, what are you talking about?" "*Mmm huh* I bet." "Why was he trying to look in here to see if you were awake on his way to the bathroom this morning?" "I don't know?" Kim said, with a grin. "Maybe he was just trying to see if I was ok." "I bet," Stephanie said. "Oh, you gone tell me" she says. Kim smiled in walked away looking back over her shoulder saying, "there is nothing to tell." Although, that was the truth; there wasn't anything to tell, just the fact that Stephanie thought there was provided all the excitement Kim needed. Kim winks one eye and recites another one of her poems.

Running Away in Time

Silver line in a grey cloud, mysterious scents with sources Unfound. A ground made solid to shake with the wind. Domination of the prayerless child whose skin I can't live in. Searching for a truth to a University of captivation. Spins as a top full of sensations. Lost in a never-ending battle that was not your own. Wishing for a path that would lead to home. Doctored by the same person that is you. For the knowledge of a distant understanding an aborted clue. Running fast as the wind even speedier than light. For running away in a time that deserved an untailored fight. Walking backwards through the scene that emulated you as you run away in time just to make through.

"Wow!" Stephanie responds; "you are truly nuts." As she leaves the room quickly lowering her head to miss the pillow which was now airborne from Kim's bed. At 9 o'clock Kim's aunt and uncles showed up refreshed for another day of travels to handle funeral arrangements for her father. This time they were all going to head over to the funeral home. Kim volunteered to go with them but, her mother insisted that she spend time with her friends and relax until the viewing. She followed her mother's directions because it never crossed her mind that she would have to go and view the body until that very moment in which the words were spoken. Kim said, "ok" with a half-smile praying not to break down in tears in front of her friends. She sat down at the table next to Stephanie and across from Fredrick. Stephanie looked at Kim as she said good morning to Roger and Fredrick. She then grins as if to be saying, "I know something is going on." Kim looked at Stephanie then at Fredrick and smiled as he tipped his glass at her. *"Mmm huh"* Stephanie's grumbles under her breathe. The breakfast was incredible. Kim thought to herself, she ate her mother's cooking all the time. However, this morning it just seemed to take her taste buds to new heights. The waffles were moist and so full of soft plum blueberries. The eggs were soft, tender and golden; the bacon was crisp and flavorful the food seemed to explode into a medley of delicious flavors as she chewed very slow enjoying every morsel. Kim and her friends made plans to hang out for a few hours before they were due to head back across town. They cleaned up the house, rolled away the fold up bed, the boys freshened up as Stephanie showered and change into some of Kim's clothes. Stephanie and Roger made up an excuse to disappear as Fredrick and Kim cleaned up the kitchen. Kim washed, and Fredrick rinsed. They talked about everything from life, death, dreams and wishes. Kim couldn't believe that in the little time they had spent together she had shared things with him that it had taken months for her to share with her closest friends. For some strange reason she felt really close to him. He was a real gentleman he never tried to hit on or touch her in a sexual way. In fact, he just really seemed to enjoy her company and she enjoyed his. Fredrick was very attractive and if Kim was going to choose a person to spend her time with she would want it to be someone like him. They talked and talked, and they were really connecting. They discovered they had a lot of the same interests and cared about some of the same things such as world peace, change, art, poetry and romance novels. When it was time for her friends to leave Kim looked around for Stephanie and Roger. Of course, they were in the bathroom with the door locked. She knocked on the door *boom! boom! boom! boom! boom! boom! boom!* "Stephanie Olivia Denise Strom you and Roger better not be in there disrespecting my mother's house!" "Of course, we aren't Roger was still hunger so I was giving him a snack before we hit the road." She bursted into laughter as she opens the door revealing that she was merely helping him bust pimples on his face. They all laughed and headed towards the front door. "Oh wait!" "I need to leave my mom a note to let her know where I am going just in case she comes back before I do." "O.k. we will meet you in the car;" Stephanie says as they all head for the door. When they arrived in St. James City Stephanie dropped the guys off. Stephanie and Kim drove to her house where she called the other girls over to meet them. Naomi, Lucy and Mia all made it over to Stephanie's house about 2:30 pm to complete the mob squad. They hung out for a few hours talking about life and how precious it is and how they wouldn't know what to do if they were in Kim's shoes. Kim didn't mind expressing herself for some reason she felt that it was now her time to break down and face her father's death head on and who better than her girls to be there to support her.

The day of the viewing Stephanie, Lucy, Mia, Naomi, Kim's aunt and uncles drove over together to give Kim and her mother some time to deal with their emotions. Kim and Mrs. McMillan talked, laughed and cried as they rode over to the funeral home. They reflected on the kind of man her father had been. Upon their arrival to the funeral parlor there were many of Mr. McMillan's friends from work and family members from all over and who else to be the first one at the door waiting to get in but ol' noisy cousin Bertha. "Look!" Mrs. McMillan stated; pointing toward the entrance of the funeral parlor door. "Boy, I tell you this woman don't miss a beat." Kim walked to her mother's side of the car and grabbed her hand; "come on mom we gotta deal with this." As tears streamed down her mother's face Kim could feel her pain and as much as she tried to be strong for her mother she felt her own emotions getting the best of her and she too began to cry as they walked towards the door. It felt as if someone had poured cement around her feet and it was beginning to harden with ever step. At one point she felt her mother tugging on her as if to say keep moving. The funeral home director explains to the two of them upon arrival that if they didn't want to do it at this time they could wait and view the body after everyone was gone but her mother insisted that they were going to do it and they were going to do it now. Kim didn't know why but as she looked at the funeral director the thought flashed across her mind about how the people that work in funeral homes always look like they were dead. She had to refocus and regain her composer because her mother needed her as they slowly approached the casket Kim could see the terror on her mother's face as she halted. Her Uncles quickly stepped up and grabbed her mother's hand as Kim's aunt Sasha took her hand and embraced her and walked slowly behind her mother. As Kim and her mother finally reached the casket she looked down at her father and begins to weep like a newborn baby as Mrs. McMillan turned to her brother-in-law Nate and questioned why? Nate embraced Mrs. McMillan and provided the infamous "God knows best," phrase. Then it was finally Kim's turn to see her father as she and her aunt walked up to the casket; initially Kim thought it was all just a dream, and then she imagined her father just lying there asleep. Finally, she reached in to touch his hands and they were so cold. His face expressed a very peaceful emotion. She reached in and touched his face it was stiff and cold, and his cheeks looked as if they had been stuffed with cotton. As the tears rolled down her face her aunt tried pulling her away and her feet wouldn't move. She wanted to walk away but her feet would not allow her body to move. Suddenly Kim's mouth opened, and words were coming from them, but Kim couldn't hear herself as she spoke. She never heard her own words, and in her mind, nothing was clear she blacked out for a moment only to come to and hear words amplified three times over. She began telling her father that she was there and that he needed to get up "wake up daddy!" "Wake up daddy!" "We miss you!" "Daddy please don't leave us, we need you!" She didn't know when or how she was pulled away but shortly thereafter she could remember being rocked in her mother's arms like a newborn baby crying. She heard Stephanie, Naomi, Lucy and Mia ask if it was o.k. for them to come in the director approached her uncle Danny and asked if it was ok to let them in and he nodded in response to say yes as they ran to her rescue. The viewing was full of her father's friend's family and co-workers whom had all come to show their respects and to offer words of consolidation regarding whatever they thought about Kim's father. It was also the first stage in the healing process for Kim and her mother. The night before her father's funeral was long, and she couldn't sleep. Kim's aunt Sasha was staying the night to provide comfort to Kim and her mother instead of at the hotel. Her aunt slipped her mother sleeping pills as headache medicine around 8:15 pm to assure she would sleep through the night. Kim pulled out her notebook and began to read a few poems to her mother as she dosed to sleep.

My Heart Needs

My heart needs a man that will stand up and be proud of me. A man, to hold my hand during my most impeccable time of need.

My heart needs a welcome mat where the road and the sun meet. It longs for the comfort from a lonely drive home surrounded by peace. My heart needs an ear on days when I want to talk. A partner to share my path on a day when I need to take a walk. My heart needs air to allow my lungs to breathe. When the intoxication of hatred and pain has all but consumed me. My heart needs a hand to touch in those spots that others can't reach. Surpass the hurt of physical pain way down deep beneath. My heart needs a piano on day when I want to sing. My heart needs a higher power much higher than the eye can see. My heart needs the Lord on the days I no longer what to be. My heart needs clear thoughts to build up strength in me.

My heart needs knees when standing becomes too hard for me. My heart needs strength to sustain the inevitable pain that was meant for me. My heart needs glory on days when my mind just wants to be. More than all the rubies, diamonds and gold the Lord is what my heart truly needs.

Every Day Is New

I see your face all the time, but every day is new.
Seventeen years together passed but every day is new.
Disagreements forgotten, grey skies turned blue.
Forgetting hurtful moments because every day is new;
I hunger and thirst for a quiet moment with you;
just because time is sweet, and every day is new.
Joined together under the Lord's mercy a union of two;

just because he knew for us every would be new.
If I didn't know your heart, couldn't read your mind
or find solidarity I would be inclined; cease to love, to live and
breathe because every day is new. Long walks in the park,
sweet smells of dew. I love the life I live as I spend
time with you. You're vigorous and fantastic and my
heart still pines for you. All because of the state of being
makes every day new.

After the second poem Kim glanced down at her mother who was completely asleep, and she decided that now was the perfect time for her to exit. She gently kissed her mother on the forehead. She eased out of the bed and crept down the hall ever so quite not to wake her mother and aunt. She picked up the cordless phone and slipped outside so no one would hear her talking. She pressed in all the numbers and prayed that Fredrick would be the one to answer the phone. "Hello," she said in a soft whisper; "is Fredrick home?" "This is he;" the voice on the other end responded. Bingo! She got lucky. It was Fredrick. "Hello, did I wake you;" clearing his throat? "No, what's wrong?" "I couldn't sleep, and I really needed someone to talk to." "Oh, ok" He was fully awake now. "Talk to me I'm listening," he said using his best psychiatrist voice. "I'm just thinking about tomorrow, you know it will be the last time I will see my father's face." "I don't think I can deal with this, it's hard you know?" "I feel like I need to be strong for my mother but what if I can't even be strong enough for myself?" "This is a really hard time for you and your family, don't beat yourself up." "You have so many people around you who love you and your mother and no matter how you feel they are going to be there to help you through it." "Yeah, your right;" she says. "I won't hold you up, thanks for listening." "You're welcome, anytime." "Good night."

"Good night beautiful." "What," but the line went dead. "Did he just call me?" "Damn;" she thought! Kim wished she could call him back and ask him what he said. "Awe, oh well forget it;" she thought. She knew to face the day which lie ahead she needed to get some sleep.

The day that seem would never arrived had finally approached as Kim and her mother prepared to be taken to the church by the limo her aunt and uncles made all the last-minute arrangements for the rest of the family that had flown in, drove up and rode down for this devastating occasion. As they proceed to the family car Kim felt someone touch her hand. As she turned to look around she saw Fredrick mouthing the words; "I'm here for you." She gave him a smile to said, "thank you" and got in the car with her mother. On the way to the funeral the family discussed the kind of man they all knew Mr. McMillan to be and how he would have been extremely pleased with the turn out. When they arrived at the church there were people standing around outside with tissues in hand crying and consoling one another. Kim clenched her mother's hand as the car rolled to a stop and glared at her with tear filled eyes and asked, "mama are you ready?" Mrs. McMillan took two deep breathes and responded; "yes baby, I'm as ready as I'll ever be." With the assistance of her two brothers-in-law Mrs. McMillan exited the car and Kim with her aunt closely in tow. As they walked towards the entrance of the church the sounds of *"I'll Fly Away"* became very over powering stirring up all the emotions that both Kim and her mother were trying to keep concealed. Walking down the aisle seemed to become more difficult with every step. At one-point Kim thought she witnessed her mother being dragged down the aisle by her uncles. As her mother finally made her way around to the casket and broke down completely. Kim's nerves totally became unraveled. She began to shake and breathe heavily as she watched her mother tell her father that she loved him and gently kiss him on the lips. Kim slowly walked up to the casket and at that moment she felt a strong hand on the small of her back whispering in her ear, "tell him, let it out, it's ok beautiful he is still with you in spirit." That was the motivation she needed she bent down kissed her father's cold harden lips and told him she loved him, and he would be forever missed. As Kim turned to look at the face of the hands that were holding her she fell into the open arms of Fredrick. His embrace was warm like a blanket on a cold day, it was soft like a cashmere sweater, and he smelled of Baron and just for a brief second that moment he made Kim feel as if all was well.

After the funeral days seem to run together and the weeks seemed to be shorter than a New York minute. After about four months her mother decided to take on another job to keep busy and to keep her mind off the passing of her husband. Kim knew her mother didn't need the money because her father had a well-paid pension package. He had the retirement years invested in his job and out of respect for his memory the Ashford County School Board awarded her mother full benefits. That along with the pending lawsuit her mother had against the insurance company that insure the driver that caused her father's untimely death. They were doing well so there was no other reason that Kim could see for her mom to take on an additional source of income. Kim began her final year in High school and things seem to get harder as the months progressed. Kim barely attended any of her classes. She thought some of her teachers were passing her out of respect for her father although he didn't teach in their county everyone knew him and loved him dearly so of course his death affected not just the county in which he had taught but in the county in which they lived as well. During her senior year Kim became very detached and she rarely saw her friends or even her own mother. When she came home from school she would go to her room and shut the door barely coming out to eat and only coming out faithfully on a routine basis to shower. Throughout it all her orderly existence and tenaciousness not to quit attending school allowed her to graduate. On the day on her graduation Kim was waiting in line for the coordinator to tell her where to stand when she got the strangest feeling like she was being watched. She turned and looked behind her and there amongst a crowd of excited graduating teenagers was Fredrick Addison. He was wearing a black jacket with patches on the elbows, a royal blue turtle neck shirt, denim Dickie blue jeans which were cuffed at the bottom and a pair of black old school suede shoes. He looked the part of a psychiatrist. He walked up to her and slowly leaned in to embrace her. "Congratulations;" he said as she nestled in his embrace taking in a deep sniff of his cologne. If there was one thing to which she could count on it was the way Fredrick smelled. He always smelled like he had just traveled to Paris. "So how have you been?" "I've been living one day at a time;" Kim responded. "What are you planning to do with yourself after this very liberating experience called graduation?" "I'm not sure, I know college is definitely in my future yet which one I'm not sure." "I have a bunch of acceptance letters at home I have to sift through." Fredrick stands back and laughs; "Naw mama calm down I'm talking about tonight." "Oh, I don't really have any plans, my mother and I are supposed to go to dinner afterwards but that's about it." "That's cool;" he responded. "Hey, listen if you're not doing anything afterwards how about you stop by the Town Center Hall?" "My parents have rented the place in honor of my brother graduating and are throwing him a party." "It's going to be fun and beside your entire clan of girlfriend's is coming." "I don't know;" Kim responded. "Maybe I will," Kim said; "if I am up to it." "Ok no pressure I hope you will consider it." "I would really like to see you there," he said. Later that night Kim decided to stop by the Town Center to socialize with her friends for she knew that this might be their last big hoopla before they go off to college. Kim arrived around 10:30 pm. "May I take your coat?" She turned around to look and it was a young man standing behind her with a ticket in hand offering to check her coat. "Yes, thank you;" she responded. As she took off her coat and the light glistened off her dress for brief second it seemed as if all the eyes in the room were on her. She was wearing a white and gold satin Dolce and Gabbanna dress which hung low around her shoulders with a wide v cut down the back which ran all the way to the small of her back. She looked radiant; she carefully scanned the room for familiar faces or at least someone she could converse with to help loosen her feeling of claustrophobia. Then from across the room she catches a glimpse of none other than her friends clustered together at the punch bowl scoping the room like hens in a coop. "Honestly ladies I thought you would all have found another approach to finding prospects." The girls truly overjoyed at this point by her presence enough so to ignore her comment as the all embrace in a group hug. "Dang Kim we we're hoping you would come girl we really do miss you and we didn't want to go off to college without getting together again for one last Pow Wow!" "Well never fear Kim is here;" she stated as they all laughed. "Ok girls let's just enjoy this night and make the most of freedom as maturing adults before reality begins to kick in;" says Mia. "I agree," says Lucy as they all proceed to the dance floor. As the night proceeds the D.J announces that he is taking final request and before next song begins to play the D.J announces: "This is a special request by Fredrick going out to Kim get close ya'll it's time to slow whine." The girls all turn in look to Kim as she turns around and notices Fredrick standing behind her with his hand out. "Ms. McMillan do you mind if I have this dance?" They all begin to clap as she gladly accepts. He slowly leads her to the middle of the dance floor pulling her body close as she leans in and says softly; "I don't know how to slow drag." "It's Ok" he says "I gotchu." Their bodies were so close you could barely see where one began and the other ended as they dance close and slowly to Musiq's song: *Love Don't Change.* "I don't know what this all means right now but this feels so good;" she softly whispers in Fredrick's ear. "It's all good just go with it;" he responds. "I just feel so comfortable with you." He then grabs her face and gently kissed her innocently on the lips. His lips were so soft and warm Kim couldn't resist she leaned in and invited him to kiss her again this time she was willing to exchange his passion. She opened her mouth allowing him to taste and savor the flavor of her minty breath as she inhaled the sweet smell of his breath which tasted like peaches. Before they knew it, they were wrapped in each other's arms going at each other like a married couple in a romantic movie. Suddenly Kim felt a tap on her should and there behind her stood Stephanie and the rest of her friends with glaring eyes and opened mouths. "Ya'll need to get a room." Too embarrassed to respond they looked around the room to peering eyes and hand claps of congratulations. "I'm sorry," he said. "I didn't mean to get carried away." "I would never disrespect you like that;" he said. "It's not your fault you didn't do any more than I wanted you to." "I think it's time for me to leave anyways," she says. "Do you need a ride?" "Sure." Kim walks over to her friends and says, "I think I am going to call it a night." "I will see you all later." "Goodnight," they all chant. "Don't do anything I wouldn't do," Stephanie adds. "They haven't invented what you wouldn't do," Kim states jokingly. On the way to Kim's house Fredrick and Kim discuss college and her plans. "Would you like to get something to eat?" "Nawl I'm not hungry." "Would you like to go for a drive?" "I'm sorry, I just don't want this night to end," he says. "Sure, we can go for a drive." They pull up to Mallman Point overlooking the Westside projects. Kim "I really do like you and I have felt this way ever since the first time we met." "I don't know what it is about you." "At first, I thought it was pity because of the death of your father." "I realized later that it wasn't that." "I mean the way I feel when I am around you is so hard to explain and when I am not with you I think about you all the time." He grazes the side of her face softly and gently he draws her chin to turn her head to face him as he continues. "I know I am four years older than you, but I really do care for you." Kim looks at him in his eyes and she leans in and they share a hot and heavy moment. He draws her body near as he begins to rise. "You don't have to do this," he says. "I know, if it gets to be too much I will let you know," she says. He begins to slowly caress her body and press his full statute manhood on to her leg. She reaches down and caressed him feeling his length and girth she begins to feel a little unsettled. "Wait," she says! "What have you changed your mind?" "No. I... I have never, I mean I am a..." "What baby you can tell me anything," he said. She looks at him with tear filled eyes. "I'm a virgin and don't know what to do once we... you know." "It's ok I'll talk you through it." He then opens his wallet and pulls out a condom. "Fredrick did you plan on doing this with me tonight?" "What?" "No!" "If you are having second thoughts baby we don't have to do this;" "I have all the time in the world to wait for you." "No, I'm o.k. I'm just a little scared," she says. "Don't be I will be very gentle." He leans her seat back all the way to an almost flat position then he slowly lowers himself on top of her. Breathing very heavily he begins to slowly insert as she flinches from the pain. "*Sssss*, oh wait!" "Wait!"

"Wait it's hurting." "Ok," he responds. "Listen take a deep breath and relax. Kim tried to relax but every time he inserted the pain was entirely too much to bear upon the final try he broke through as she screamed and begin to peel the skin off his forearm. He kissed her softly on the fore head and wiped her tears as he moaned. She began to shake underneath the pressure and then she pushed forcefully asking him to stop. He slowly slid out notices that the condom had broken and there was a small collection of semen inside. He figured he was almost at a climax. He didn't realize in all his desire he secreted. At her request he complied as he released a long-drawn sigh of anguish. "Did we just," she asked? "Ahh physically yes, technically no," he responded. "Are you upset with me," she asked? "No baby," he responds. "Come on let me take you home." As they drove to Kim's house there was complete silence. Kim sat thinking about what and just happen as Fredrick sat thinking about what didn't happen. Upon arrival to Kim's house she thanked him for a very interesting night and he promised to call her when he arrived home. Kim walked in the house and quietly crept past the couch which her mother was laying fast asleep. She didn't want to wake her and have her ask how her night went because she was almost certain that she would have to lie. She grabbed her pajamas and quickly went into the bathroom. She discovered that her beautiful and very expensive Dolce and Gabbanna dress was ruined. There was blood all over it. As she explored her body she questioned: "Did I just get my period?" As she showered she wipe constantly to see more evidence to support her theory but there wasn't any. "What has happened to me;" she thought? After showering Kim climb into bed and waited for Fredrick to call and it never happened finally she drifted off to sleep. The next day Kim awoke to her phone ringing off the hook she looks down at her alarm clock it was only 8:30 am. She wondered who could be calling this early then she thought; "it must be Fredrick." She dived across the bed and answered only to hear Stephanie's voice on the other end inquiring about her happenings from the night before. "So, girl did chu give um some?" "Good morning to you too Stephanie." "Why are you calling me at... glancing the clock, 8:33am?" "So, did cha, did cha, did cha, did cha?" "Would you hush; you sound like a broken record." "You my dear are being evasive." "I know you gave him some on his last night before he gets shipped off." "Huh what are you talking about shipped off?" "Fredrick has been in boot camp for six months and he is being shipped off today at 4:00 pm for a 12 month stretch in the Marines; I thought he told you?" "No, he didn't;" Kim replied.

As time went on the girls all chose universities of their choice and everyone went off to college. Years past and Kim and her friends seemed to lose touch as they matured and chose courses of study. After two years of community college Lucy, Mia, Naomi and Stephanie all wound up at the same University. *Seven years later...* Kim returns home from college. "Kimberly McMillan is that you?" She heard a voice from behind her as she sat waiting on her mom at the bus station. Kim slowly turned around to see Roger standing there. She hadn't been home that much in seven years and she could barely recognize his face he had certainly matured and grown from puny to his brother's identical twin. It had been seven years since she had seen any of her high school friends and she didn't know if they would all look the same for from the looks of Roger he sure didn't. Through hazy glances and desperate reels of confusion wow those honey brown eyes and the snow-white smile; it truly was Fredrick's younger brother Roger, the heart throb of Stephanie's life. "Hey Kim, I haven't heard from you in a while." "I asked Stephanie about you and she said you hadn't been home since three months after graduation." so they hadn't seen you in a while." "How are you?" "I'm ok, just needed some time and space to think about things," she explained. "Oh, I understand completely, can I give you a ride somewhere?" "Nawl, maybe some other time, I'm waiting on my mother." "It's ok I can drop you off at her job come on I don't mind." "I am on my way to pick up Fredrick from the airport anyways, so it wouldn't be out of my way." "I don't mind honestly." Kim's skin crawled at the sound of Fredrick's name she felt so betrayed and disgusted by the thought of how he left without a noted or so much as a phone call after she gave him the very fruit of her being. "So how has he been," she asked? "Who Fredrick, oh he is doing well." "He finished his degree in Psychology in the Marines and saved all the money he earned to come home and open his own private practice with none other than his baby brother." "Wow that's great," she responded trying not to reveal the hurt in her voice as she spoke. "Come on let me give you a ride it's the least I could do for you since you haven't been home in what seems like forever." Kim agreed, and they drove up town towards the Community Service Tower or CST building where her mother worked doing clerical work. "So, is this your car?" "Yup." "This is a nice car, BMW wow; you are truly coming up in the world." "So where did you get it?" "I am in the process of buying it from Campbell's Auto Mall." "I put two thousand down on it three weeks ago sort of an early pre-private practice gift." "So, what you been up to lately?" "Nothing much, looking for a place to put my law degree to work." "Yeah so is everyone else; all your girls attended the same college and are now searching for jobs." "Where did you go?" "Berkley Academy of the Arts 7 year double major program," Kim stated. "Wow, Kim you go girl!" "Hey, listen we have planned a big party tonight celebrating Fredrick returning home from the Marine Corp I hope you will come?" "I don't know; I haven't seen any of the old clan in years." As she thought to herself; "Fredrick is the last person I want to see right now." "That's all the more reason to come tonight if you ask me?" "Here is the address hope to see you there." Kim's return home was truly a surprise welcome to her mother. Mrs. McMillan looked as if she hadn't aged a bit she looked radiant glowing smile and strong tall stance she was the same strong black woman Kim remembered her being when she first left for college. She and her mother went out for lunch and they were playing catch up when she announced to Kim that she had some news to share with her. "Kim baby, I … I kind of met someone." "What!" "What do you mean you met someone?" "I mean that I have met someone; his name is Kenny and we have been seeing each other for about eight months now." "So… I don't know what to say this is all a surprise." "I don't know what to say ma." "I would like for you to meet him." "Ok" she stated hesitantly. "When is this endeavor to meet Mr. Kenny scheduled?" "What about tonight?" "Oh, I don't know about tonight, ma I just made plans to reconnect with the girls." "It's only for a few minutes Kimmy we are not going to hold you up from hanging with your friends." "Alright ma I meet Mr. Kenny." It was great to be out again hanging with the girls, Kim thought but she still felt like something was missing things were very different for her now the good times were just memories in her mind and although the girls were trying hard to rekindle the excitement flame of friendship in their lives which had once been, Kim still seem to be distant. "Group hug!" the girls yelled as they all ran over to Kim as she entered the party. "I am so glad you decided to come tonight Kim." "Girl we really missed you;" said Stephanie. "Yeah, I just thought I would come out for a little while." "Girl, it's a lot of cute guys in here;" said Mia. "Yeah, I guess so." "Come on, get up on your feet and dance!" "Nawl, not right now Mia, maybe later." "What's wrong with you?" "Nothing I just found out my mother is seeing some man named Kenny." "Oh Mr. Kenny I know him he is really nice Kim you need to give him a chance." "I don't know about all that." "Ok then what about dancing?" "Nawl I'm good." "Ok but you are going to get up before the night is over." "Yeah alright." As the night went on Kim begin thinking of a good excuse to exit the party when she looked across the room and noticed a guy with a very familiar face standing there watching her. As he began to get closer she started searching her mind for a reason to walk away although she thought that if see ever saw his face again she would kill him she knew that in her heart she still had feeling for him. He was her first and she wanted to know why he left her without a word. "Should I ignore him, she thought?" "Should I walk away?" As he approached she could see his glowing white smile and very seductive lips and her body trembled. "Hey beautiful, how are you?" "Huh?" "Are you talking to me;" Kim says as look behind her? "Yes of course;" he responded as he gently grabbed her hand to kiss it. "If it isn't the beautiful Ms. Kimberly McMilllan?" "Hey…Freddy what's up?" Trying to play off the fact that she had been feeling betrayed by him. "Fredrick the name is Fredrick." "I know I was just playing." "Ha, ha, ha" "So how long has it been?" "Seven years, three months, twelve days and eight hours," she responded. "Ok, so how have you been?" "It is what it is; you know, just taking it one day at a time," she responded. "I don't mean to be rude, but do you have a date and if not, would you like to dance?" "Nawl I'll pass, or do you not remember what happened the last night you and I danced together?" "Come on this is my favorite song; I would love to dance with you while listening to it and besides it wasn't even like that." Melting into his glowing bright smile she could no longer refuse. As Fredrick coached her onto the floor with his one hand high in the air he yelled, "yeah;" the D.J must have read my mind." "Do you believe in omens?" "*Mmm huh*," she responded. "I believe this song was meant to play at this very moment." "What do you think?" Kim gave him a flirtatious smile as she and Fredrick danced to Jamie Foxx's *Unpredictable*. As his strong hands grabbed the small of her back she melted in his arms. The two of them danced close and slow as Fredrick sang in her ear with warm sweet breath that smelled like juicy ripe peaches. Kim melted in his arms and closed her eyes tight as she tightens her embrace and smelled the nape of his neck which was lace with the sweet smell of 99 Roca Wear cologne. After the dance they talked, laughed, and took in a mental stroll down memory lane. "You hurt me ya know?" "I waited all night for you to call me." "I felt so stupid." "I'm sorry baby, it wasn't like that I didn't want to hurt you by telling you I had to leave after we…. Ah you know." "When I called back looking for you it was too late, and you had already left for college." "I never told anyone what happened between us because I didn't want anyone in our business." "Oh, so we have business now," she says. "I thought you would be married with kids by now." "No, you were all I could think about." "Yeah right for seven years, get real!" "Listen I'm not looking to be hurt again, I think it's time I call it a night." "Wait!" "Kim can I at least have your number?" "Why because you want me to sit up all night waiting for you to call like when I was a young teenager in love?" "What, nawl come here let me talk to you…please?" She walked away and promptly exited the party.

"Hello," Kim answered. "Hey girl you still up?" Dang, she thought; 'yeah I'm awake what's up?" "Oh, nothing I just wanted to know if you wanted to go with us tomorrow to the step show on 750 Belmont?" "I don't know I might, I will holla at you in the morning." "Ok good night." Again, the phone rings Kim dives across the bed to answer. "Hello?" "Hey beautiful what's up?" "Nothing, what is up with you and how did you get my number?" "Please who are you kidding your mother's number hasn't changed in over the past seven years and besides the number is listed." "I am surprise you are still awake." "Yeah I am normally up until about ten o'clock." "So, can I take you out for lunch tomorrow about one o' clock?" "Um I am supposed to meet up with the girls tomorrow for the step show on 750 Belmont." "Ok what about dinner?" "Why?" "Look Fredrick, I don't have time for your games." "No but I feel like I owe you an explanation; can you at least give me that?" "Please that was over seven years ago and besides I was young and I'm not holding a grudge." "Nevertheless, let me get this off my chest I need to apologize and tell you why." "Sure, that sounds good." "What time would you like to meet?" "I can pick you up about eight?" "Make it eight thirty and you got a date." "Ok good night sweetie." "Good night." "Yes, yes, yes!" She shouted as she hung up the phone Kim was excited about being able to possibly rekindle the flame and the chemistry that she once felt for Fredrick. Kim loved the way Fredrick made her feel when she was with him. She had to tell someone about how she felt and who better then Stephanie. "Hey Stephanie!" "What's up I thought you went to bed?" "No, I'm still up." "Listen, what do you think about Fredrick?" "Cedrick who, oh wait a minute did you say Fredrick?" "Roger's brother Fredrick?" "Yes, I like him." "He seems to be pretty cool." "Why, are you planning on hooking up with him?" "Maybe, ugh!" "I don't know. I got to think I will call you later." Fredrick was a very nice and gentle person who Kim saw herself being able to fall for him. After the show Fredrick decided to meet up with Kim and her friends at the step show and take her out to dinner from there. They talked, and he explained all that he had been through during his service in the Marine Corp. He explained to her that even though he had left she was always a constant thought in his mind. They seem to pick up their relationship right where they left off and Kim became very content with what their relationship was beginning to become.

It was a very hot morning so hot Kim could feel the covers sticking to her body as she rolled out of the bed thanking God, she had made it to see another day. Just then the phone rang in of course who else but none other than Fredrick was on the line. "Hey beautiful what's up; whatcha doing today?" "I don't know yet I haven't made any plans." "What are you up to?" "Nothing much, how about you and I go get some lunch say about 1:30ish?" "I have someone I would really like for you to meet." "Wow! Ok does he want me to meet his mother she thought to herself?" "Am I ready for this?" She questioned nevertheless she agreed. "Great, he said." "I will pick up around 11:00 am." "Whoa why so early?" "Well I have a surprise for you and it is going to take us a while to get there". "Ok well give me about 45 minutes I just got out of the bed." "Ok no problem see you soon, take care beautiful." "Bye Fredrick." Her heart begins to pound so hard it seems as if it would come out of her chest. "I have to wear the perfect outfit don't want to seem to trashy nor do I want to seem as if I have no flavor when I meet his mother because first impressions are very important," Kim thought. Kim turned on the radio as she began to look for her perfect outfit to meet Fredrick's mother. About an hour later Fredrick rings the doorbell. Kim opens the front door dressed in a sleek and sultriest Vera Wang satin V-neck black dress accented with gold accessories. "Wow!" Fredrick states, as he looks at her from head to toe. "You look beautiful!" "Thank you," Kim replied as she steps back through the thrush hold of the door way with a smiling invitation for Fredrick to come in. "I just have to grab my shawl and I will be ready." As she walked away Fredrick took note of every inch of her body from her long silky-smooth legs, up to her round plump apple bottom, small sleek waist, and perky sized 38C's. Kim slowly walked to the room down the hall almost certain that Fredrick was watching as she walked away slightly glimpsing behind to catch him staring as she walked away she grabbed her shawl from the bed gently and slowly lacing her neck, breast, and mid-section with her favorite perfume "Usher" for women. She slowly walked down the hall coaching herself through the very tense moment she felt was ever before her on this trip to his mother's house. "Ok I'm ready." "Alright let's go," said Fredrick as he stood to his feet to open the door. As she moved he watched her every detail. He opened her car door and quickly strides to the driver side and they were off. "Are you nervous?" "Don't be my mother is very sweet and she has been waiting to meet you." "Do I look Ok?" Kim stated, as she fixed her shawl to be sure not to reveal too much skin. "No!" "You look better then O.k. you look beautiful." Kim gave him a big smile as she stepped out of the car. A little boy darted from behind the fence yelling, "they're here!" "Aunt PegSue they're here!" "That's just my little cousin Damien," Fredrick stated. "How many people are here?" Kim began to question as the noise from the house picked up the closer they got to the door. "Oh, just 35 people or so we are having sort of a family gathering," he said. "That's my surprise I wanted you to meet my whole family." "I talk about you so much they have all been waiting to meet you." "Wait, what do you mean we have only been seeing each other for a few months how could they know so much about me already?" "Maybe that is the way you see it but the night we all met on the courts was the first time you and I started seeing each other." "Sure, there have been several years since then, but you are all that I have spoken of since that time and my family was beginning to think you were a myth." "Roger knew I was in love with a girl, yet I never revealed your name because he would have told Stephanie and of course she would have told the entire world." "I didn't tell you how I felt before because I always knew I wanted to go into the Marine Corp and I didn't want to start a relationship with you before leaving because that wouldn't have been fair to you or me." "This way there would be no pressure on you to feel obligated to wait for me when I went to the Marine Corps." "The way I figured it, if it was meant to be, you would be single when I got home and true as the day is blue you were." "So, you trying to tell me you had this whole thing planned since the day you saw me at the party?" "No, it's nothing like that what I'm saying is you were the one I had in my heart." "So, what are you saying?" "Truth be told I love you; I have always loved you since the first day I met you." "I just never said anything because not many people believe in love at first sight." "To be honest I didn't even know what I was feeling." "Wow that is a lot to take in," Kim said. "I know and I'm sorry to have to break it down to you like this, but I didn't want you to think this was something I do often." "You know how some guys are bring chicks home to meet my mother every Sunday." "You don't have to do this if you don't want." "I am more than willing to excuse myself and take you where ever you want to go." "No, I am fine I just never knew how you felt and hearing it all now it's just overwhelming." "I always had thoughts of you and I knew that within me there was something more to us then just friends." "I never wanted to over step the boundaries to what I might have interpreted as feelings and it was merely friendship." As he took her hand and kissed it she could feel the warmth of his breathe on her hand and the tenderness of his lips which conveyed to her that he was sincere in his intentions for establishing a relationship with her where completely honorable. As they entered the house everyone welcomed Kim with open arms their where three generations of Fredrick's family all under one roof laughing, talking, playing, and sharing remember when stories about times past. Then finally at the end of the long trail of relatives was his mother. She had a smile that could glow up a night sky and the skin the color of creamy caramel. Her hair was shoulder length and shinier than a new penny. She reached out her arms to embrace Kim and kissed her on the check. As Kim stood welcoming the warm embrace of Fredrick's mother she whispered in Kim's ear "baby you are a God send." Kim didn't know what his mother meant by those words but sooner than later she was going to find out. Then she felt a strong pair of hands grab her around the waist and whip her around; it was Fredrick's father Mr. Addison. "Hello lovely lady I am none other than the father of this here striking lad you call your boyfriend." "If he ever gets out of line you let me know and I will take him down, because I taught him better than that." After meeting his family and enjoying all the delicious food that had been prepared Kim kindly thanked Fredrick's family gave them all hugs and decided it was time to call it a night. "So, did you enjoy yourself tonight?" "Yes, I did, and your folks have a beautiful home." "Thank you, most of those things you seen on the walls and inside of the cabinets are artifacts my mother and father brought back with them from Egypt." "So how long were they over there?" About 10 years total their research and findings have been published in a book titled, The Riches of the Night." "Wow!" "That's deep." "Yeah, they really enjoyed what they were doing, and it has been really inspiring for our family how they were able to go to a foreign country and discover and do things that many people before them could not." "I'm proud of them." "So, onto something I am interested in; what are you planning to do with yourself for the rest of the evening?" "I don't know I hadn't really planned anything." "Why?" "I was just curious." "Would you like to see the new place I'm looking into buying?" "It's one of those foreclosure properties that needs to be fixed up but with the money I am going to save during the purchase it will be worth it." "So, what do you say?"

"Ok, I guess it's still early." They drove down to 152nd Street and Florencedale the Street was well lit and each home on the block had a nice seven-foot fence around it. The car slows to a crawling speed and stopped. "We are here;" Fredrick said as he put the car in park. He grabbed Kim by the hand and took her around to the side of the house where the realtor's box was located. Inside the box was a key. He opened the door and began to give Kim the grand tour. To her surprise the inside of the house was in really good shape. There were hard wood floors in every room and a dual fire place which was located between the living room and kitchen. The windows already had custom made casted iron bars on them and the home had a total of four rooms, two car garage, three and a half baths, a study, kitchen, dining, and open foyer with vaulted 10-foot ceilings. "Like I said it needs a little fixing up, but I can do it." "Fredrick this is beautiful." "I love it, it is very nice." "I am glad you like it;" he said as he leaned in close staring into her eyes. "That was all the conformation I needed, this house is as good as sold." He took her by the hand and said; "let's go it's getting late and I need to get you home before your mother starts to worry about you." Kim smiled and said ok.

"Hey girl what's up I haven't heard from you in a month of Sunday's where have you been?" "What have you been up to lately the girls and I were all worried about you?" "I have been around just trying to figure out what to do with the rest of my life." Kim's friends were getting together for their weekend ritual.

"You want to come with us it will be just like old times?" "Ok let me just check things over with Fredrick and I will call you later." "You two have really hit it off and now ya'll are acting like an old married couple." "Whatever!" "I will call you after my job interview tomorrow with my final decision." "Alright mother maid!" "Ha, ha, ha you are not even cute." *Rrrring, rrrring, rrrring.* "What; who could this be calling it's four O' clock in the morning?" "Hello, who is this?" "It's me, can I come over I need to talk?" "O.K." she said clearing her throat. "Is everything O.k.?" "Is your mom, dad, and Roger alright?" "Yeah baby I just need to talk to you." "It's o.k. I'm up." "Good because I'm outside your door." "What!" Fully awake now she jump to her feet and rushed to the bathroom to quickly brush her teeth and wash her face careful not to wake her mother in the process. Tip toeing down the hall she crept to the front door. "Come in," she said in a very low whisper. "No, I can't." "Can you step out for a minute?" "I promise I won't keep you long this is very important." "What is wrong, Fredrick you are scaring me?" "Sorry baby I just need to tell you something. "I am leaving tomorrow for a few weeks I have to take care of some business and I will be back." "I didn't want to leave without telling you." "What?" "Why?" "Where are you going?" Her heart begins to pound she knew that if he were to walk out of her life again she wouldn't know if she would have the strength to wait for another seven years. "I am going to finalize the purchase of the house and then I am going to take care of something in Davenport I will return in a few weeks." "Same old Fredrick," she says. "At least I didn't give you any of my precious temple this time before you decided to walk." "Baby please it's not like that this is very important I wish I could tell you more right now, but I can't please just trust me I promise I will call you every day." "Ok?" "I Love you baby and just know that I will be back in a couple of weeks." "Ok" Kim said as she looked at him with tearful eyes. "Awe baby please don't do this to me I am a man but I ain't above crying." "I don't ever want to see you hurting for no one not even me there is no man worth that but God." "I know," she said. "I, I, I love you Fredrick." He grabbed her by the small of her waist and kissed her lips ever so softly while holding the back of her neck pulling her closer as he started to rise and take a stand she pulled away. "Baby we can't do this now." "I know he said, I'm sorry I just lost control for a second." "I didn't mean to disrespect you; this is not what I came for." "You don't have to apologize." "I'll save myself for you!" "I'm proud of you. That's great!" "Why are you so excited, she asked?" "Huh nothing, I mean now I have no worries because no other man can try to steal you away from me while I am gone." He laughed as she looked at him with despising eyes. "I'm just kidding baby, but I promise I will be back sooner than you think" "I will call you every day." They shared another passionate kiss and said good night.

By Myself

Follow a path down to its end to see where it will take you only to know that it is not taking you far enough for you to get through. You preach, you practice, you serve as a model of the life you lead only to find you must learn how to deal with life all by myself. Playing a round of my favorite game all by myself. Hurting from a broken heart all by myself. Being alone in the dark all by myself. Don't know where to go or who to turn to on the hardest day of my life all by myself. Waiting for a miracle all by myself.

Kim had a very strange way of dealing with her emotions. Everything in life seemed to have a story or some significant play of words she deemed poetic. Canted recaps of thoughts intertwined by the state of mental romance which she saw as an emotional unhinging to a noted past time. The next morning Kim woke up feeling as if she had won the lottery. As she crawled out of bed she felt a little different she looked down at her hand and there was a 4 carat Winston Herring Diamond engagement ring on her finger.

She looked down on the night stand and there was a note written in small script: Will you make me the happiest man in the world? Kimberly McMillan will you marry me? "How could he?" "When did he;" she thought. "Ma!" Ma!" "What!" "Look, look at my hand." "Girl where did you get that?" "Ma you trying to tell me you had nothing to do with this?" "Girl I have no idea as to what you are talking about;" Mrs. McMillan stated as she walked over and hugged Kim with a big grin and said; "congratulations baby." For the remainder of the morning Kim could be heard throughout the house singing Brandi's rendition of *Missing You.* "Kim!" "Kim!" "Girl what's wrong with you I have been calling you for two minutes in all I can here is this racket." "Who are you missing?" "Huh?" "No one ma, I just like that song." "O.k. yeah right, we'll let that girl who gets paid to sing it sang the song until you leave my house today?" "I can't hear anything in here." "Yes ma'am," she said as she laughed her way to the kitchen. "Oh yeah before you go Fredrick called and said he will call you later around four O'clock." "He did?" "Mm huh like I'm crazy; ain't missing nobody my foot, girl do you think I was born in a card board box?" "Alright ma me and the girls are going to go over to La La's I meant Lucy's house to hang out." "When Lucy bought a house?" "I meant Mr. and Mrs. Fugal's house." "Alright baby you be careful out there on that road." "I will mama. I love you." "I Love you too baby." It was about one O' clock when Kim reached Stephanie's house. "What's up girlfriend mmm huh you tell me you are the one

with all the little well-kept secrets huh whatcha talking about?"
"You know what I am talking about you and Fredrick." "Oh well
I didn't know if it was going anywhere so I just waited until I
knew if it was going to be something." "Besides I knew Roger big
mouth but was going to tell you anyway." "Yeah but nevertheless
you should have told me." "Ok so you going to be mad at me all
day or what?" "Nawl, I ain't mad; disappointed is all." "O.k. yeah
right, like the time you told us about the girl that was trying to
creep with Roger that one time." "Oh, that was different." "Yeah
here you go with the double standards again." "Anyways, where
are we going?" "Well everybody is supposed to meet up at Lucy's
house and we are going out from there." "Ok let me grab my bag
and I will be ready to go in about twenty seconds." "Oh, let me
say good bye to mom's and pop's so, they don't go off." "I still
can't believe that in a few months we will all be attending you
and Fredrick's wedding." As promised Fredrick called every day
until he returned. Upon his return he explained to Kim that
during his serve in the Marine Corp. He witnessed some illegal
code of ethics violations between two of his superiors which
had to be kept confidential until after their trials. After sharing
the news, he explained to Kim that therefore he had to leave
so suddenly and that he couldn't tell her for fear that someone
would find out, then he too would be brought up on charges for
leaking confidential government information. Upon his return
Fredrick bought a small office in town and began his practice in
the field of psychiatry almost immediately.

Kim loved Fredrick so much, but she was afraid she had
not told him that she was keeping a very hurtful secret buried
deep inside. But she figures that he would understand, so she
made up in her mind that she was going to tell him tonight.
The anticipation was increasingly growing inside of her. Instead
of waiting until that night she figured she would drive over to

his office and surprise him and get the full experience of lying on his big leather couch and experiencing what the rest of his patients experienced. She arrived at Fredrick's office and she waited patiently outside until he was finished. Kim had signed in as a patient and was waiting to be treated as such. Fredrick opened the door without looking out into the waiting room he looked at the name on the list with a puzzled look ah, um… "Mrs. Addison" expecting to see his mother, as Kim stood to her feet. "Oh, baby you know you didn't have to sign in to see me, come in." "Debra please hold all calls and visitors until further notice." "Yes Sir," Debra responded. "What's up baby?" Kim lay down on the leather couch and said, "Baby I have something to tell you." "Ok," Fredrick responded. "I, I, I" Kim sat up on the couch with tears streaming down her cheeks and begins to pour out all the details about the night she vowed to never relive. During her third year of college on the way to her dorm from the library Kim had been sexually assaulted by an unsuspecting person. She explained she had been dating a very nice young man named Mike who was the casting director for the Art intern program. He called her earlier that evening to break off a date he had with her. She told him that she would then go to the library and get some studying done. On her way back from the library she took a route she most commonly used to short cut her way to her dorm in 10 minutes. Although it was still earlier many of the people who were normally out that night had went home for the Labor Day holiday weekend. She explained right before the attack she remembered feeling a sharp pain in her lower back and she blacked out. When she came to she could smell the fragrance of English Leather cologne and alcohol. Her assailant had restrained her legs with shoe laces as she struggled to get free. He promptly punched her in the face twice with two solid blows to her nose and mouth as she begged him to release her.

She screamed with fear as the pain of the blows rushed to her face. She cried out for help praying that anyone would hear her as her attacker then placed a dirty sock in her mouth. Her hands were securely bound behind her back as she wiggled around like a fish out of water trying to keep him from violating her. This only made him angrier as he grabbed her a begin ripping her clothing from her body. A slither of light trickled through the trees allowing her to see overhead. The area was unfamiliar to her and she realized that she was no longer on the college campus and that her attacker must have carried or drove her away after knocking her unconscious. With terror in her eyes she thought to herself; God please let this be a dream. She soon felt the gut wrenching pain of her attacker violating her temple. He was very violent in the manner of his attack brutally forcing himself inside of her in leadership and follow-up positions repeatedly for 2 hours. Kim felt as if someone hand taken sand paper in rubbed and scraped her insides out. Upon completion of this attack he stood over her and laughed as he proceeds to soak her with discarded remnants of alcohol while she lay in the fetal position crying like an abandon infant. Crying hysterically at this point she continued explaining to Fredrick that he then cut off the restraints and just walked away into the night leaving her to find her way back to the main highway and walk the 4 miles back to the campus scared and humiliated. She remembers returning to her dorm trying to wash off the stench of the attack. She refused to share her horrific ordeal with anyone including Mike. She was too embarrassed to call the police in report the incident and too afraid. She withdrew from Mike and looked at him with such terror and fear any time he tried to show any signs of affection. She became very withdrawn, broke off her relationship with Mike and decided to check herself into a mental hospital for suicidal victims. She the deadly disease that was killing thousands of young African Americans every year. "Good morning Kim the doctor will see you now." It seemed like forever before Kim approached the door she slowly turned the knob and took a deep breathe. "Well hello Ms. McMillan it is good seeing you again." "So how have you been feeling lately?" "Ok I guess." "Doc if you don't mind I would like to cut past the small talk and find out the results of my test." Although those were the words that came out of Kim's mouth she really didn't mean it. If fact she was quite frightened and the anticipation of not knowing the result clouded her mind into speaking. "Ok then, I completely understand." "I must say though before I reveal the results regardless of the outcome your life is precious at any state and is worth living and you have plenty of options as far as help for getting through the aftermath." "Yes, sir," she responded. "Your test results revealed....," Kim sat down in the chair crying becoming overwhelmed with emotion. Dr. Floyd with a concerned heart stop speaking. He pulled a chair close to Kim and spoke. "Kim, I realize that you have a lot to deal with right now and if you want I can set up an appointment to see a psychiatrist friend of mine she is really good." "No, thanks." "Well the results have revealed that you are all clear." "You did not contract Aids nor the HIV virus strand of Aids, congratulations!" "I do hope that you will seek professional help for dealing with your mental afflictions." "Thank you so very much Doc." "May I have a copy of my results?" "Sure, stop by the front desk on your way out and ask Shirley for a copy." Kim gladly celebrated her results with Fredrick. They were soon married shortly thereafter, and they moved into their new home.

Fredrick became very productive at his psychiatry office and Kim was preparing to make partner at one of the most well-known firms in town. Despite the buzz flying around the office

Kim kept her guard up and continued to work just as hard on every case. She was very dedicated to her job and to her husband. She was always home by five O' clock to prepare a hot meal. After all that she had been through, her life finally begins to feel complete. She and Fredrick were planning to establish a nice six figure nest egg before having children and they were very close to their quota estimating another year or so before they would settle.

It was a Friday afternoon and Kim were just wrapping up with her last client getting ready to head home when she got this sharp pain in her hip. "Whoa!" "Are you ok Mrs. Addison," asked Mr. Malika the door man as he opened the door to let her out. "Yes, Mr. Malika could you please have the valet pull my car around?" "Yes ma'am Mrs. Addison." "Ouch;" she yelled as he quickly turned to assist her. "Are you sure you are alright?" "*Mmm* I think so, it's probably just stress." "I will soak in the tub and try to relax when I get home." "Thank you, Mr. Malika, have a good weekend." "You too Mrs. Addison."

That afternoon Fredrick arrived home looking very tired. Kim was standing in the kitchen preparing a nice candlelit dinner. "Hey baby, are you ready for dinner or would you like to shower first?" "Give me a minute baby I'm going to go shower and then I will meet you at the table in 15 minutes." "Ok," Kim senses a distant and withdrawn vibe coming from Fredrick. She turned the stove off and proceeded to enter the bedroom when she heard him talking on the telephone. "You know what I can't deal with this right now!" "I told you before stop calling me when I am home!" "You should have taken care of that situation four years ago!" With a puzzled look on her face Kim pushed open the door. "Is everything Ok baby." "Huh?" "Uh, yeah just a client wanting to know if they could schedule an appointment last minute." He grabbed her around the waist and kissed her then slowly and seductively making a trail from her chin down her neck to her shoulder and gently nibbling her neck while slowly sucking blood to the surface of her skin. Pushing her slowly towards the bed and delicately unbuttoning her shirt. Just as the phone rang "ignore it" he whispered in her ear. She flips open his phone and saw the name Heather she quickly closed it and mentioned that the food was getting cold as she pushed him off her. "Ok I see how you are." "You won't even let me grind on you huh?" "Hurry up beside your boys, the ladies, and we are supposed to go out tonight." "Nawl baby ya'll go ahead I'm in for the night." "I got a busy day schedule for tomorrow." "What!" "Tomorrow is the weekend and the office is closed." "Come on baby I just have a few files that Debra forgot to put vital information in, so I must straighten them out to make sure it is done correctly this time." "It's not her fault we got this new system we…" Just then the phone rang again. As Kim walked over to pick it up she could see the name Heather flash on the caller I.D. as Fredrick reached over to mash the receiver. "Why did you hang up the phone?" "It is after hour's baby I don't have time for all that nonsense." "You go hang out have a nice time and tell them I will catch them on the rebound." It was at that moment that Kim's woman's intuition kicked in and she decided to concoct a plan to prove her heart felt theory.

It had been six weeks since the Heather's phone calls and Kim began to assume that she in fact had over reacted. Kim's phone rang she looked at the caller I.D. and it was Stephanie. "Hey girl what's up?" "Nothing much what are you doing?" "I need your help really quick how fast can you get to the Smart Mart on 87th Ave about two minutes?" "Why?" "Girl I got a flat and I need a lift hurry up, you know people down here are a trip about leaving your vehicle." "Ok I'm on my way." Kim pulled in the parking lot to see Stephanie sitting inside her car parked in the back in the shadows sitting low under the steering wheel. "Girl you better have a flat tire somewhere on this car or I'm going to flat one for you making me drive over here for nothing." Just then Stephanie says nothing and just points in the west direction across the street where Fredrick was standing with a little boy about four years old that look so much like him you would think that he gave birth himself. There was a woman sitting inside the car with the word Heather on the windshield. Kim's heart begins to pound so hard and heavy you would think it was literally going to beat out of her chest. She had to keep her cool because she did not want to make a scene. Filled with angry, confusion, and hurt she headed for home to call Fredrick to see what his excuse would be for his whereabouts. Upon arriving home, she picked up the phone to dial his number as he was walking through the door. Before she could hear the second ring she heard the key in the door. "Hey baby how was your day?" "Great how was yours?" She pretended to be excited as usual to see him it took everything she had in her to keep the smile plastered on her face. "Good despite all the traffic," stated Fredrick. "So, did you get off a little later than normal today or did you stop off somewhere?" "Yeah I got off late and I stopped by my home boy's house for a minute to see if he was home." "Why didn't you just call him on the phone?" "What's with all the questions Inspector Gadget?" "Nothing I was just curious." "I know you are normally home by now I was a little worried that's all." "Well I'm here baby, I am not going nowhere." "I have a surprise for you as she slowly unbuttons the top of her shirt." "Are you serious?" "Yeah, I'm going to go take a shower and I'll be right back." "Ok I'm going to go pour us something to drink." Fredrick walks to the kitchen as Kim quickly grabs his cell phone from his coat pocket she goes into the bathroom and press redial. The phone rings on the second ring a woman answers; "hello baby are you calling to tell your son good night?" "Hold on"; a small voice on the other end says, "hello, daddy?" Kim quickly hung up the phone. It begins to ring as she turns the phone off and tosses it on the bed. Kim hears Fredrick's footsteps coming down the hall. She runs to the bathroom and begins to cry silently into a towel to muffle the sound as she shakes uncontrollably. Thinking to herself "how could he do this?" Kim decides she was not going out without a fight and the most vindictive revenge for his wicked ways of indiscretion would be the ultimate payback of her own. As she showers Kim thinks of a way to carry out her plan without causing further hurt to herself. Then it hit her, she remembered hearing about a woman who used super glue to teach her husband a lesson. Kim thought about this plan as her sufficient plan for payback to Fredrick for the pain and the hurt of his indiscretions. As she prepared for the moment she laced her skin with sweet scents of intention and hot oils. She glossed her lips with Victoria Secret strawberry lip gloss the kind that tasted like strawberries when she licked her lips. She then put on her two-piece black open cut Victorian laced negligee with matching black stiletto pumps. She walked into the shadows of candlelight reaching for the play button on the stereo the music begins playing a slow mix of all the latest bedroom mixes ever made. She danced slow bending over; touching her toes and moving just right allowing the silhouettes to cast traces of her body on the wall. She moved in closer and closer to Fredrick's body until she could feel her skin rubbing against him. She gave him a nice slow lap dance allowing him to trace her zenith of her breast with his tongue as she grabbed his head shoving it forcefully into the pit of her bosom. She rose up and down cradling his head then she bent back his neck and lick a trail down to his six pack abs where she began to unbutton his pants with her teeth breathing heavily that was higher than any other. Kim went to church that Sunday morning to not only recommit her life to Christ but to also release all the devastating issues about her life to the only one willing force who could take on her life's struggles. After the sermon the door of the church was opened for all those who were willing to come onto Jesus for rest. Somewhere in between asking for prayer and confessing her problems to the pastor Kim had been noted kneeling for a period of eight minutes before she was then shaken and awaken by her mother with tear streaked cheeks and a host of her Christian peers. She had willfully confessed an entire life of terror that would never be forgotten. Kim had been raped, she never completely got over her father's death and the one person she had fallen in love with betrayed her. Because of her mental state of destruction, she decided she thought she was no longer fit to live. Kim finally decided she was going to make choices about her own life and no one would ever hurt her again. Later that day she decided to check into a hotel because she couldn't face Fredrick or her mother. *Rrrring… rrrring*, "Hello?" "Hello Mrs. McMillan, have you seen Kim I need to talk to her?" "Why haven't you hurt her enough?" "Listen Fredrick I don't normally get into ya'll business, but I think right is right and wrong is wrong!" "You had no right to lead my daughter on and marry her if you knew you were still going to play the field." "Hold on Mrs. McMillan let me explain, Heather is not nor, has she ever been my girlfriend." "I just recently found out I was adopted, and I was raised by the Addison's as their own child." "It wasn't until I was in the Marine Corp that I learned about my twin brother who was killed in the line of duty." "When I found out he had a wife and kid I went down to meet them and pay my respects." "When I went to Heather's house she explained to me that she didn't have the nerve to tell their four-year-old son his father was dead."

I Should Have Known Better

The Sequel to The Force of Life's Confession

Silvia was confused she wanted to follow her heart, but her mind led her to believe that if she gave up all her material possessions and moved away to Colorado she would never recover all that she would be leaving behind. Four years ago, life was far less complex than it had become now, and she was sure that it would become even more complex before she deplaned. The hazy image of the past four years began to play back in her mind as she sat looking out the window of seat C3. She remembered the day she sat staring out the window of her luxurious office on the 57th floor of Carver and Carver an Executive Marketing Firm. She reflected on her life and the possibilities of what changes would derive from starting over. *Buzz*, the sound of her desk phone interrupted her from her long-perplexed stare out the window. "Ms. Goshin you have a call, Mr. Paul is on line two." "Thank you, Janice," she replied. Silvia had been dating Paul for two years and she really loved him. However, she always felt as if something was missing from their relationship. Paul was 6'5 220 lbs. of pure muscle. He was a health guru and loved to hit the gym during his free time. He was very handsome with nicely trimmed black hair and goatee. His smile reflected fine porcelain with beautiful perfectly straight teeth that were glowing white. Every time she saw him her heart would skip a beat. Paul had the kind of personality that made any woman love to be his accompanist. Slightly engulf in thought Silvia picked up the phone. The strong baritone voice on the other end speaks; "hey honey, how are things going at the office?" "Everything is well, thank God," she replied. "Great!" Paul replies, "but you sound a little melancholy." "Anything you care to talk about?" "No, not really, just some things I have on my mind I need to take care of." "Ok, just as long as you're alright." With a sonic burst of energy in his voice Paul states; "would you like to go out to our favorite restaurant on Fresno Avenue tonight?" "Sure," she replied; "how does nine o clock sound?" "Great, I will meet you there." Although Silvia and Paul had been dating for two years Silvia had made it very clear early in the relationship that she was not looking for a commitment. Paul loved Silvia with all his heart and often couldn't understand her preservations regarding their relationship. Nevertheless, Paul had so much respect for Silvia. Her decision to remain independent and secure was fine with him and he never questioned her motives. He simply complied with her wishes. Paul knew Silvia's story regarding her past relationship. She met a guy and fell in love putting her whole heart in soul into the relationship. They build a home together with the intentions of spending the rest of their lives together. She loved and cherished him only to find out 13 years later that he had used her, cheated on her many times, and destroyed their marriage. He put her out of their home. He assumed he and his mistresses would have a terrific life together. However, he was sadly mistaken 2 months after she was out of the house his mistress lost interest and moved on leaving him high and dry. She learned that he later moved to a different country to pursue a career in music. She knew within herself that all of this was wrong but out of the love and respect she once contained for him she never fought or asked for one thing she simply walked away. She vowed to never let another man into her heart again. As the healing process began she truly found the strength of God to release and let go of the pain. As they continued talking for a few minutes Paul suggested he would like to come by and pick her up for dinner and she abruptly stopped him in his tracks. "No, thank you!" "I will meet you at the restaurant." "Ok baby," he replied. "I just wanted to treat you the way you deserve to be treated." "I will talk to you later." "I love you," he said, as she quickly hung up the phone to keep from having to respond. "Janice!" "Yes Ms. Goshin, can you get Mr. Malcolm on the phone he is number 21 on the call log?" "Yes ma'am," she replied. *Buzzzz,* it was Janice on the line. "Ms. Goshin, Mr. Malcolm is on line one." "Thank you, Janice;" she said, Silvia cleared her throat as she picked up the phone using her very professional and sophisticated voice. "Good afternoon Mr. Malcolm, this is Silvia Goshin." "I was just returning your call." "I apologize for not returning it sooner I've been extremely busy." "I completely understand," said the seductive and strong voice on the other end. Silvia's heart began to pound rapidly as if to almost beat out of her chest. Just the sound of his sultry voice made her feel like a school girl with a crush. Trying not to think about what he looked and smelled like the last time she saw him. "I was calling to R.S.V.P for the class reunion." "Great," he responded sounding cheerful. "How many people will be accompanying you?" "I'm not sure at this point." "Could you please forward the information to me at Carver and Carver Marketing Firm in Norfolk Springs, Virginia via fax?" "Wow!" "You work for Carver and Carver huh?" "That's impressive!" "Yeah well, I worked hard enough to get here, and they treat me well." "That's great, well I will send the information out immediately." "I look forward to seeing you at the reunion." "Ok, I will talk to you later Ms. Goshin." "Ok Malcolm she replied, take care of yourself." Silvia sat at her desk tapping her pen on a file that needed to be attended to; she released a big sighed and reflected on Malcolm her first love from Colorado Springs. She used to be so deeply in love with Malcolm. She hadn't seen Malcolm since she went off to college over 15 years ago. She had heard rumors that Malcolm became a successful business man in Colorado. Silvia wonder if Malcolm still looked the same tall, sleek, and handsome his build and statue was so close to Paul the resemblance was staggering. Reality set in when the phone buzzed again it was Janice informing her that her 2:30pm appointment had arrived. "Ms. Goshin, Mr. Richards is here for his appointment is it ok to send him in?" "Give me five minutes and then send him in." "Yes ma'am Ms. Goshin." Silvia quickly powdered her face and walked towards the door. She had been noted by her colleagues as the Marketing Firm's unrivaled queen because she worked with and landed the companies top marketing clients. Most of her clients were billionaire business owners. She was in fact the best person man or woman around in the marketing venue and her bosses were aware of her skills. She received a hefty salary of two-quarters of a million dollars per year with paid vacation, benefits and sick leave which she never took. "Good afternoon Mr. Richards," she stated as she opened the door. Mr. Richards reached out and grabbed her hand with a firm shake as she peeked around the corner and informed Janice to hold all calls and visitors until further notice. This is a code four which was their secret code for Janice to tell any of the bosses who dropped by unannounced that she was in the middle of landing a marketing deal. Mr. Richards was a multi-millionaire who earned his fortune selling small micro-chips which are installed inside computer modems to make them automatically kill and wipeout computer viruses. After approximately 45 minutes Silvia and Mr. Richards immerged from the door. "Stop by the front desk and schedule a follow up appointment with Janice." "If you have any questions before that time please feel free to call me, she said." No one could ever figure out how she did her job so well and she had become the envy of everyone at the office. Silvia was very methodical in her work and no matter what she always seems to get every client she encountered to sign with her marketing firm. She knew that if she left and moved back to Colorado whoever was going to replace her would have some big stilettos to fill. As the day progressed she continued preparing portfolios and going over some last-minute details and sketches for products on the marketing lineup for her clients. Silvia always worked diligently to complete all files that were on her desk before the closing of the day. Silvia had spent most of her time convincing herself that nothing in the world was worth her emotional and mental attachment other than God, family, friends, and her job. She shut down her computer and began to mentally plan for her date with Paul. She always followed a strict regimen of eight hours for work, eight hours for sleep, and eight hours for leisure time. She knew that anything that didn't align with this schedule must be dismissed from her life. "What should I wear," she thought as she walked towards the elevator? She envisioned the little silver and black elegant gown she had in her closet which had been design exclusively for her by J.D. Madeeds. He was one of the best designers in the Virginia area and she felt the need to always have the best and the top of the line in fashions even if it meant having clothes made by designers who hadn't realized that they were already famous. The thing about Silvia was that she prided herself on not conforming to any direction or model in which the world had carved out for her. She had been that way for years and she worked hard to stay on wooden nickels or play the fool for anyone anymore. Even though she felt this way she continued to pray to God and petition him to speak to her inter spirit of discernment and strengthen to heal her from past failures and hurt. Based on past occurrences in her life all the people she allowed to enter her heart and trusted seemed to hurt her. She had no intentions of allowing anyone else to ever hurt her again. It was still a little early in the evening when she completed the half hour drive to her luxurious five-bedroom four bath Dominican waterfront home designed by the Trolly Brothers. As she approached the massive black and gold titanium and steel iron casted gate she envisioned an evening of soaking in a nice hot bath and reading a nice romance novel as she waited for her date later that evening with Paul. She arrived at the door with a greeting from Wilbur, Burberry and Flounder. "Hey, babies did you all miss mommy today?" They all tried to jump in her arms at once. "Wait a minute let mommy put down her things," she stated. As she rounded the corner to check the mail bin she notices one of her very expensive signature bowls with sterling scribe costing $1,100 had been broken. With a look of total disgust, she tried to maintain her composure as she questioned; "Which of you broke mommy's bowl?" Wilbur and Flounder looked at Burberry as she dropped her head and whimpered. "Awe Burberry," she stated; "didn't mommy tell you to stay out of the comfort room when she is not home?" Burberry whimpered some more as she made an apologetic motion and then quickly retreated to the time out corner which contain a nice cashmere doggie bed and T.V and a timeout clock in which the dogs were all trained to push with their nose to start the timer whenever they were sent to the time out corner. "Now mommy is going to have to take away your allowance for two months to replace the bowl you broke." She walked over and kissed Burberry on the nose and stated, "but mommy still loves you." She then looked at the clock it was already three minutes after five. She called down to the guest house and asked Mrs. Barnstine to feed the dogs and clean up the crystal. Although she had a maid, the maid was not allowed inside of the house unless Silvia was home which gave the dogs free run of the house until she returned home. The dogs received food and daily walks from Mrs. Barnstine based on a timing system which would go off certain times of the day a loud and very disturbing high pitch dog whistle would go off signaling the dogs to go outside using the doggie door and walked across the pond to the guest house where Mrs. Barnstine would be waiting for them. Mrs. Barnstine didn't mind she received free room and board. She ate the best foods, earned bonuses, and paid vacations on top of her salary. She had worked for Silvia for seven years. Mrs. Barnstine didn't have any family in the states and after her day was over she was at liberty to do as she pleased. Mrs. Barnstine loved her life and had recently acquired a boyfriend. Mrs. Barnstine having a boyfriend was very admirable. Silvia viewed Mrs. Barnstine relationship as rejuvenating because it gave her a sense of comfort knowing that there was still hope for her to settle down later in life if she decided. Silva remembers the first time she saw Mrs. Barnstine sneaking her boyfriend into the guest house. She unintentionally over heard them having a late night quixotic moment. Silvia didn't mind in fact she thought it was rather cute that a 62-year-old woman could still have the stamina to interact in an affectionate, passionate, lustful, and intimate relationship. Silvia remembered four years after Mrs. Barnstine's husband passed away Mrs. Barnstine who has a very strong Russian accent asked her where she could get some condoms. Holding back laughter she remembers driving her down to the pharmacy and watching Mrs. Barnstine spend fifteen minutes looking at all the sizes and colors before she chose the right ones. The buzzer went off on the timer next to the tub which signals she had a little more than an hour to get ready for her date. She walked into the closet in her bathrobe pushed the button and the clothes began to rotate around until she found the perfect outfit. She picked out a red and black Maidan Hattox Niteline Ruched gown. The dress was beautiful, sleek black, which had a nice v-neck drop, and a thigh high split in the front with a reversible red and black shawl and matching red Dior patent pumps. She accented her neck with a gold omega necklace with a ruby pendent and matching earring. She pulled her hair back into an elegant clamp. She applied lipstick, makeup and a few squirts of Prada perfume and headed for the door. Burberry had now been released from the time out corner in just enough time to receive a goodnight kiss along with Flounder and Wilbur. "Goodnight gang mommy loves you and don't wait up mommy has a date with Mr. Paul." Whenever she went out on dates she would always hire a car service in the event she wanted to really enjoy herself with a few drinks she would not feel obligated to depend on Paul to take her home and try to spend the night. Everything in life had to make sense to her and there had to be a logical reasoning behind everything. When she arrived, Paul was waiting at the door. The driver exited the car and approached the back-passenger door and opened it. Paul walked up to the door and grabbed her hand as she exited the car to ensure her safety he stated, "you look ravishing." "Thank you very much," she replied with eloquence in her voice as her deep dimples and radiant smile accented her perfectly made up face. Silva was 5'9 170lbs with an hourglass figure which men enjoyed viewing as she walked passed. Her smile was like a soft white light bulb which was nicely accented by her deep dimples and smooth mocha colored skin. As they proceed to enter the restaurant he placed his hand in the small of her back, asserting ladies first. As they walked into the foyer of the restaurant they were greeted by Flex the restaurant host. "Good afternoon Mr. Paul and Ms. Silvia," he stated in his very strong French accent. "It will be my pleasure to seat tonight." Silvia love to hear Flex speak she smiled at him as she thought to herself I need to schedule my next vacation in Paris, France. The night was beautiful as usual, and Paul was a sensational date. He was always so intriguing, and his conversation was intellectual. As she sat looking at her lobster brisk she thought to herself "why can't I commit to this man he is such a great person and very attractive?" Silvia knew the answer to her question and in fact if she was to verbalize the truth to Paul it would surely destroy their relationship. She knew things about him that created a wall of distrust that made her secretly compared him to her past marriage and she would not love him fully because of the hurt. The ambiance in the restaurant was beautiful. The lights were low, food delicious and the music was soft and romantic. Paul was a mysterious and romantic guy he seemed to know everything Silvia felt, and he could read her so well. He stared in her eyes as he stated, "Ms. Goshin may I have this dance?" Silvia smiled very seductively as she grabbed his hand. Paul led her to the dance floor and pulled her close. They danced so slow and eloquently as he held her with the embrace comparable to a precious rare diamond. He slid his big strong hands around her small and delicate waist as he began a slow two step close sinuous dance accompanied with an 80-degree grind mid-section to mid-section. The dance was not provocative just slow, sinuous, comforting, and elegant; a dance of lovers. Silvia wondered how he learned to dance so well because all the men she ever knew could never in a million years dance the way Paul did. As she was wrapped up in thought he whispered in her ear. "I could live like this with you in my arms forever." Realizing what had just been stated she stared at Paul as if he had just asked her to marry him. "What do you mean you could live like this forever?" "I just mean that this feels so right that's all don't get all frayed out by that statement." "I just want you to know I am deeply, madly and passionately in love with you." "Oh, ok," she said. "Tell me something;" Paul responded, "why are you so afraid of commitment?" "Paul, I don't want to talk about that right now." "Besides we are having such a wonderful time why ruin it." "I'm sorry," he replied. "I never seem to be able to reach the inside of you." "Why are you always so guarded?" "What must I do to win your trust?" "I know that I have earned it!" His voice got increasingly louder. "Paul please, lower your voice," she stated. "Ok Silvia, whatever you want." "Why don't we just say goodnight now and start fresh tomorrow." "That sounds good," she replied as she gently kissed him on the cheek and return to their table to pay the bill. They summoned the waiter to bring the bill and as they sat quietly staring at one another he with curiosity and she with worry. Paul quietly walked Silvia to her car door as the driver opened it. He reached down and kissed her on the lips and said, "good night my queen." "Good night Paul," she stated as he closed the door and her car drove off in the distance.

Silvia woke up to the sounds of three yelping dogs. Good morning babies, she stated as she peeled back the purple and black satin sheets and comforter. Burberry, Wilbur, and Flounder walked up the doggie steps into bed licking her face as if she was wearing makeup made of kibble. "How are you doing?" she stated in a voice in which grown-ups often use when talking to children. "It's time for breakfast!" She pushed the button to call out to the guest house and asked Mrs. Barnstine to prepare breakfast for the dogs. Silvia's Morning ritual consisted of a granola bar, fresh fruit, a glass of orange juice and yogurt. She would run four miles every morning with the dogs and workout for approximately an hour before the crack of dawn. Silvia had been able to control every minute of every day of her life. Whenever the thought of her losing control would cross her mind she would become flighty meaning she would run away from the situation or circumstance. By eleven o' clock she had been able to complete her entire routine and watch her favorite show with 45 minutes to spare. She reached over for the phone and pressed number two on the speed dial. "Hello, hey mom!" "How are you?" "I'm good baby but this old arthritis has me down in the bed, but I am alive in well, so I won't complain." "So, how are you?" "I'm good mom just wanted to check on you." "You don't sound alright." Silvia sat wondering. "How can she do that?" Anytime anything was bothering her, her mother always knew just by the tone in her voice. "I am fine mother she stated with assertiveness." "Ok, so what are you up to this weekend?" "I don't know I was thinking about just lounging around and not doing anything for the whole day just getting some rest." "Yeah you need to rest because child you are always on the go." "I know mama I'm always busy." After her mother made her promised to slow down in life and take some time to come visit her she hung up the phone. Silvia began to reflect on her life. Silvia's life was unlike what many people thought. It was very dark because of the mental scars that she had endured from her past she kept them hidden in her mind. Each day she prayed for strength to become stronger, better, and wiser. She prayed for a forgiving heart and unconditional loving spirit towards those who had hurt her. Silvia looked at herself in the mirror. I need a vacation she said as she looked through a brochure for exotic vacation spots. *Hmm* Belize sounds nice. Seven days in another country with such beautiful scenery. She turned to Wilbur, Burberry and Flounder and said; "what do you think?" "Do you think we should all take a family vacation to Belize?" Burberry turned her head sideways as if to say let me think about it and Silvia laughed and dropped to the floor rolling over and pretended to wrestle with them on the floor. "Alright... alright," she says as she kisses each of them on the nose. Mommy must take a shower and get ready. "You all watch T.V. I will be right back." All three dogs walk up the doggie steps to the bed and lay quietly on the bed waiting and watching T.V. as they were ordered. The one thing Silvia knew more than the color of her own hair was the loyalty of her dogs and their level of consistent obedience. Just as she steps out of the shower the phone rings. She pushed the speaker button to answer. "Hello, hey honey what's going on with you," the voice on the other end states? "Nothing much, who is this?" "Oh, so you have been in the bat cave so long you don't even know the sound of your own friend's voice." "Ok, I have several friends;" Silvia responded laughing because at this point she was merely toying with her. "I know who this is what's up Gina how are you?" "I am good." "Listen the girls and I was all thinking about going out to the health club today about 4:00 pm." "Do you want to come?" "Sure, who's going?" "Sara, Maria, and Brenda are going." "Ok." "We are doing a girl's day out." Silvia quickly responded, "Yes, Lord knows I need a spa day." "I need a little R and R." "Ok we are going to meet at Gerod Jewelers at 3:00 pm so Brenda can drop off her ugly 3 karate diamond ring to get her initials put inside." "Awe don't hate on Brenda she so deserves to be happy and in love." "I am so happy she has found Mr. Act right." "Some men can be the most traitorous creatures." "Yeah, so can women!" "Anyways, enough of that." "I will see you ladies in a few hours." "Hey why don't you bring the car, so we can all have a good time, and no one will have to drive home?" "Ok, I will call now and have them pick you all up along the way." "Thanks Silvia,"

Gina replied. Silvia then packed a small gym bag and put on a pair of snug Ed Hardy skinny jeans, knee high Prada boots, a tight Dolce Shirt and matching vest. As Silvia proceeds to go down stairs she pushes the voice box to the guest house on the wall and summons Mrs. Barnstine to the big house to gather the dogs and put them in the doggy party room. This was a small house which had been specially designed for the dogs approximately 200 square feet of luxury located in the right corner of the yard equipped with air conditioning, refrigerated water, individual doggy toilets, a 27-inch flat screen T.V. and precooked steak bits for the dogs so Mrs. Barnstine would not have to bother with them. The doggy party room is much like a small apartment equipped with beds, toys, and all the amenities for the dogs. On her way out, the door the phone rang. "Oh, who could this be, she thought?" "Hello, good afternoon, may I speak to Ms. Silvia Goshin?" "This is she." "Hello, you don't know me, but my name is Fredrick I am the husband of Kimberly McMillan." "Oh, wow ok how is Kimberly I haven't heard from her since college?" "We were best friends and as thick as thieves." "Is she ok?" "Well that the thing, see there has been sort of an accident." "Is everything Ok?" "Um… no ma'am I am sorry to be the one to tell you this, but Kimberly died this morning." "What!" "No!" "What happened?" "Well um, she um, she um committed suicide." "Oh God No!" "I am sorry to have to call you with such bad news however, I was going through her address and phone book and I found your number." "I didn't know how close you two really were." "However, I figured if your name was listed in her book she must have cared for you enough to write it down." "I'm sorry we were not able to meet under better circumstances." "That's ok, is there anything I can do?" "Do you need assistance with arrangements?" "No ma'am her mother and I will be discussing that in the next couple days."

"Is there anything I can do to help?" "No, not currently." "I will stay in touch and call you when the final arrangements are made." "Ok, listen I will be on the next flight out I will see you soon." Silvia sat down on the floor as Mrs. Barnstine proceeded to enter. Mrs. Barnstine ran in the room when she noticed Silvia dropping to the floor. "Is everything ok?" Silvia asked her to call and cancel all her appointments. She informed Mrs. Barnstine that she would need her to stay in the house with the dogs for a few days because she was preparing to leave on a trip for the funeral and she would be gone for a few days. Silvia then picked up her blackberry called all her girlfriends and informed them of the news. Silvia called the office and informed her bosses that she would need some time off to go to the funeral and without hesitation it was granted. Silvia always kept her files up to date or ahead to ensure productivity and success just in case of an emergency such as this. The last call before she begins to pack went to Paul and as usual he was compassionate towards her needs and wanted to assist her by any means necessary. He asked to accompany her. As usual in Silvia fashion she refused; stating she would call him with news of funeral arrangements when she received them and that he could come then to console her if he wanted. He agreed and offered to drive her to the airport she complied and acknowledged that she would allow him to do so. Upon arriving to the airport Silvia begin to have all kinds of thoughts such as what would make Kimberly kill herself? She was so bewildered that she didn't even notice when Paul departed. She walked up to the gate to board the plane when she heard the words wait up. Astonished Paul was returning with one first class ticket for the same flight. He grabbed her hand and stated where you go I go. Silvia smile and secretly let out a sigh of relief. As the plane landed in Delray she looked at Paul and with a smile she stated thank you for coming I feel so much better because you are here. He smiled back stating; "it's my pleasure Ms. Goshin." Upon her arrival to the airport Fredrick was there standing in the breeze way with a sign with her name on it. They immediately embraced one another as she apologized, and he explained that Mrs. McMillan was entertaining family and friends and sent him to assure she was greeted by someone and it provided him with a few minutes to clear his head. As she let out a deep sigh she wanted to be empathetic however, curiosity was eating away at her and she really wanted to know what would make one of the strongest people she had ever met kill herself. "Fredrick, I know this is a hard time for you right now but, could you please tell me what happen?" "I just don't understand why she would do that she was such a strong person and more mentally stable than anyone I know." She could see that he was getting a little choked up, so she apologized and stated he didn't have to respond. He quietly took her up on her offer not to talk about it and headed towards the McMillan's residence. When they arrived at Mrs. McMillan's home there were already people arriving to pay their respects. "Hello Mrs. McMillan, How are you holding up?" "As well as can be baby come on in." Silva then turns to Paul and introduces him as her boyfriend which was the first time she had ever addressed him in that manner in public usually it was just always implied that he was her boyfriend, but she never verbally said it to Paul this was big. "You both are welcome," Mrs. McMillan stated; as she ushered them both into the house. Inside Fredrick sat in a lounge chair in the corner crying and shaking his head as he continued to try to explain what lead up to the suicide. Silva was so appalled by the facts that such a perplexing situation could cause someone she really admired to take her own life. For the next couple of days Silva and Paul assisted Fredrick and Mrs. McMillan with the final arrangements and assisting other friends and family find hotels and sleeping quarters while they were in town. Silvia reflected on her own life when she found out that her ex-husband was cheating on her and how she secretly tried to work it out. After a year of cheating and he still would not stop the hurt of secretly holding his infidelity inside begin to chip away at her. She became an emotional wreck. She tried to take her own life, but it was Kimberly who helped her through such a difficult time. She encouraged Silvia and motivated her to seek God and trust in only him to make her life and her situation better. She sat visualizing the conversation she had with Kimberly those many years ago about life, love, God and trust. Without warning tears filled her eyes and she became overwhelmed with grief. She shuddered to think that this could have been her those many years ago. In fact, this could have been her family preparing to bury her with grief-stricken hearts. After four days of running around and meeting more people than she cared to remember the day was rapidly approaching for the funeral. Silva looked up at the clock, she noticed that she only had about an hour before the viewing of the body. She was debating back in forth in her mind should she go or wait until the funeral. After some prompting from Paul she decided she would attend the viewing. "Are you ready?" Paul asked as she walked up to the doors of the funeral home. "Yes honey, I'm ready." Now at this point she wasn't sure if it was her nerves, the environment, or the situation. However, Silva seemed to be much more compassionate and affectionate towards Paul. Silva walked into the building and stepped into the foyer as soft music played in the background she looked towards the front of the room offset the entry way where her dear friend lay in a white casket trimmed in light purple. As she stepped closer her legs begin to shake as she turned to Paul and said, "I don't think I can do this." "I'm here for you he stated we can do this but, only when you are ready." "You can do this baby just take your time." Silva then decided to take a seat midway up the aisle. After collecting her thoughts, she proceeded once more to go to view the body this time making it to the casket. She leaned slightly forwarded and peered in. There as angelic and beautiful as the last time she had seen her lay Kimberly with somewhat of a partial smile on her face as if she was peacefully sleeping. A sudden calmness came over Silva as she stood there watching Kimberly. "She looks as if she is asleep doesn't she," she leaned over and whispered to Paul. "Yeah baby she does," he replied. She then looked up at the lining inside the casket. There a small inscription which read: "A little angel gone before his time." "What does that mean," she asked Mrs. McMillan? Wiping tears from her eyes she stated; "Kimberly was four months pregnant and it was a boy." "Oh my gosh!" Silvia was in total disbelief this could not be real. It was like she was waiting for someone to pinch her. She embraced Mrs. McMillan and said; "I had no idea." Mrs. McMillan replied; neither did we. "I don't think Kimmy knew baby." "I just can't see her killing her baby had she known." "I know she would not have done this." Silvia sat quietly staring at all the family members and friends as they walked around talking and consoling one another. She began reflecting on her own life. Silvia was not an only child although many of her acquaintances assumed she was. She had three brothers and two sisters. Silvia began to think about life, love, and family. She had never seen so many people express such love and compassion for one person. The display of love was something she knew was missing in her own family. "Are you ready?" Paul stated as he shook her gently on the shoulder because the viewing service was ending. "Yes baby," she responded. Paul didn't understand what was going on with Silvia and her recent display of affection towards him. Nevertheless, he was more than willing to openly receive it. Paul stop short on the entry way and consulted Silvia about taking everyone in Kimberly's family out for dinner that night if they were up to it. Silvia thought that it was a great idea and agreed to proceed with the invitation. Upon submission of the invite everyone apart from a few accepted the invite and agreed to meet back at Mrs. McMillan's home around 7:15pm for dinner. Paul made a reservation for the 26 family and friends of Kimberly at Jean-Puer's Seafood and Steak House Restaurant. Paul had three hours to rent two large limo buses and get ready for the night. After making all the arrangements he went back to his hotel room and called Silvia on the phone. He had left Silvia with Fredrick and Mrs. McMillan to give them some time talk. Silvia arranged to meet him back at the hotel around 5:30 pm. He called her room to tell her that all the arrangements had been made when the phone rang Silvia picked up after the third ring crying. "What's wrong Paul ask with sincere concern in his voice?" Silvia then begins to explain the story of what led to Kimberly's suicide and how a simple misunderstanding and miscommunication caused her to give up her life. Paul asked if he could come over to her room to comfort her and she agreed. His arrival came one minute later Silvia open the door and flew into his arms with a tear streaked face just wanting to be held and Paul was there to comfort her. As she embraced him like never she nestled into the nape of his neck with heavy panting barely able to speak she said; "I am so glad you are here with me please don't let me go just hold me tight." Without hesitation Paul held her tight but ever so gently. He caressed her back then grabbed her face and gave her a soft subtle passionate kiss on the lips. He looked deeply into her eyes and stated; "I am here for you for as long as you want me to be." "I will never let you go." For the first time Silvia said; "I love you to Paul and meant it with all her heart." After a phone call home to check on Mrs.

Barnstine, the dogs, and her closest friends she decided to take a nice hot shower to get ready for dinner. When they arrived at Mrs. McMillan's home the limo buses were already there. Each bus was equipped to carry thirteen adults comfortably with a fully stocked mini bar and a 50 Inch platinum TV with satellite. The family and friends were grouped according to age and all were excited because most had never been in a limo let alone a limo bus. Kimberly's closest friends, Fredrick, Silvia and Paul were in one bus and her mother, step-father, and older relatives were in the other. Despite the occasion in which the dinner represented everyone seem to have a good time. The restaurant was beautiful, the food was perfect, and the family shared many happy stories and remember when memories of Kimberly's life. Around 10:00 pm the family agreed to call it a night to prepare for the inevitable day of mourning which was quickly approaching. Everyone so graciously thanked Silvia and Paul for everything including a wonderful evening of dinner and reflection as they departed. Back at the hotel Silvia looked at Paul and thanked him once again for being there. As he embraced her she gently nestled in his neck and kissed him with her soft warm lips. Trying to contain is increasing passionate flare he kissed her on the forehead and walked her to her room. She inserted her key card stepped through the entry way and turned back and kissed him softly on the lips. He grabbed the back of her head and pulled her close. So, close she could feel the growth of his passion emerging below. With their lips still pressed firmly against each other she muttered out the words, "stay with me tonight." Not wanting to use this moment as a means of egoistic gain. He asked, "are you sure?" "Yes, I'm very sure;" she replied with a reassuring smile on her face. The next morning everyone arrived at Mrs. McMillan's home to get in the processional line which was due to arrive to the church at 11:00

am. Mrs. McMillan welcomed Silvia, Paul, Fredrick, and Kim's closest friends to ride in the three cars provided only for family. In her eyes they were more than friends and acquaintances they were family. They all agreed with her request and departed in the family cars. Upon arriving to the church there were so many people who were there it was difficult to see the entry way to the building. There was one very noticeable car parked slightly adjacent to the building. It was the car from a state orphanage with a huge logo on the side. Mrs. McMillan couldn't help but to wonder why someone would drive this vehicle to her daughter's funeral. She questioned the church officials and funeral home directors however, no one could explain. They asked that she just focus on the service of her daughter and they would find answers to her questions later. The service was beautiful. Everyone had such loving and funny stories to tell about Kimberly during the reflection time. Then there was one request made by a stranger to speak that would bring forth the answers to the questions in which McMillan had asked before the start of the service. The request came from an unknown acquaintance of Kimberly's. No one had ever known that during her days of college Kimberly worked for an orphanage not even Silvia knew about it. *Hello, my name is Mrs. Graham and I worked with Kimberly some fourteen years ago at the Oopsy Orphanage back when she was in college. Kimberly was a very smart and ambitious young lady. She helped bail me out during my time of need. It was at that moment that I decided to make her part owner of the Orphanage in which she wanted to remain a silent partner right up until this present day. She called me about two weeks ago and asked that I come down and deliver her will and other important documents. She stated that everything was ok but that it was important that I delivered them personally. It was so painful to arrive last week and learn of her death in the daily newspaper as I was waiting on her call to inform me of where to meet. If there was anything Kim could count on was that no matter where I went I would pick up the daily paper and read the obituary. I do this because although many of the kids don't know their parents I make it my business to know the biological parents of each child before they come into the Orphanage and in the event one of them passes away. I keep the newspaper until the child is old enough to search on their own for the next of kin. So quiet naturally you can imagine my surprise when I came here and checked into the local hotel and picked up the paper to find the very person who sent for me and whom I loved so dearly has passed.* As she holds up an envelope in her hand and proceeds to walk towards Mrs. McMillan please note that this paper was drafted many years before her marriage. Please read it before you leave the church today. God bless you then she quickly walks out of the church. As Mrs. McMillan rips open the envelope with all eyes on her. She read: *Dear Mom, I know this is not the way you raised me to be. However, I didn't know how else to handle my situation. After daddy died I lost a piece of my existence. When I got pregnant I never told anyone not even his father. I didn't understand how you would continue to view me if I would have kept him. So, I gave Christopher to the Orphanage. I also worked there and being part owner, I knew he would receive the best care. Mrs. Graham has raised him as her own. I loved my son more than life itself and I would have done anything to have a second chance to do everything all over again.* Mrs. McMillan was very confused as she dropped the letter to the floor and raced out the door to find Mrs. Graham who by this time has been long gone. As Fredrick read the letter he looked around and grabbed his mother-in-law's hand he said; "mom calmed down, I bet he is in here." Fredrick walked to the front of the church and spoke into the microphone. "Christopher, I know you are here." "Please come here." "We are your family and we love you." "Please stand up Christopher we didn't know you existed." "Please!" Slowly a young man stood and began to walk to the front of the church. Before anyone could say a word, Fredrick ran to him a hugged him tight with Mrs. McMillan right behind him. Silvia and Paul looked at each other in total disbelief. Mrs. Addison stood up with her hand over her mouth she walked over put her hands-on Christopher's shoulder and said, "Fredrick Christopher's your son." "What, how do you know that?" "It makes perfect sense now, I remember when Kimberly was leaving for college she asked me if I had heard from you and how you were doing." "We had this long conversation about life and choices." "She had asked me if it was possible for a person to conceive if they had used a condom." "The conversation turned strange because I questioned her about being pregnant and she laughed saying she was just joking." She asked me if I knew of the name of a good dentist near where she was going to attend college and I told her yes and she left." "I always had a weird feeling about our conversation." They look at Christopher and it made perfect sense he was the splitting image of Fredrick. "What is your full name, Mrs. Addison asked?" Christopher replied; "Christopher Fredrick Addison." "How old are you?" "I am fifteen years old." "When is your birthday?" Sure, enough his birthday was nine months to the day in which Fredrick and Kimberly made love for the first time. But "why didn't she tell me," he thought? "All emotions aside it was time to introduce Christopher to his mother," said Mrs. McMillan. "Do you want to see your mother?" Christopher shook his head yes as they all walked up to the casket. When the casket was opened Christopher dropped his head and wept. "Are you ok Christopher?" "This is Ms. Johnson?" "Ms. Who?" "Ms. Johnson at the Orphanage she said her name was Ms. Johnson." "She was a real nice lady she was always very nice to me." "I told her once that I wish she could be my mom." "I dreamed that she would take me home with her." "Now I find out that she really is my mother and it hurts." "Come on baby we going to take you home and figure this all out after the funeral." "Did you bring any clothes with you?" "Yes ma'am; Mrs. Graham paid the limo driver one hundred dollars after everyone went in the church to place them in the trunk of the car." "Ok good let's go bury your mother and we will go home." "Fredrick what are you doing on the phone?" "I am calling my lawyer to ensure that no one can take him away from me." Mrs. Addison yelled; "boy get off the phone now is not the time and I would like to see anybody try and take him." "Let's go!" "Wow," Silvia stated! "I would have never in a million years have believed this if anyone had told me and I still don't believe it." "Well believe it baby because it is real," said Paul. The revelation of Kimberly and Fredrick's son didn't undercut Kim's funeral however, the darkness of that day became a little brighter because of Christopher. Silvia and Paul prepared to return to Virginia and everyone in Kim's family back in Delray was attempting to return to some form of normalcy. Paul and Silvia were just about to board their plane when they heard a call from the breeze way it was Fredrick standing there with Christopher they had come to say thank you and to see them off. Silvia and Paul ran back to receive one final hug and to make a vowed promise to keep in touch and if there was anything that either of them ever needed for them not to hesitate to call. Upon arriving home Silvia and Paul rode together in Paul's car as they headed towards Silvia's home. Paul looked at Silvia and said; "baby you are beautiful." "Thank you but I don't feel beautiful I have jet lag and I am ready to crash." "Have you ever thought about having some children," he asked? "No," she replied, "I have three remember?" "Oh, ok well technically dogs don't count." "They do in my world and they are just as expensive," she said. "Yeah, you're right, because we all know that Wilbur, Burberry, and Flounder aren't the typical dogs and they are spoiled rotten by their mommy." "That's right," she said as they both laughed. As they pulled up to Silvia's home and Paul proceed to retrieve her bags she looked at Paul as his muscles rippled and glisten in the sun. Silvia thought to herself I could get use to this. Paul could see that something was on her mind because she didn't respond to him and she was biting her bottom lip as if someone had just invited her to taste her favorite dessert. Finally, she responded to his third call when he began to jingle his keys. "Baby are you alright?" "Yes," she replied, "why do you ask?" "Because I was talking to you and you didn't respond then I called your name several times and still you didn't respond." "Oh yeah, I'm fine." "Hey neither of us have to be to work for the next couple of days." "What do you say, you and I spend the day by the pool drinking ice cold margaritas?" "Oh, that sounds good." "Are you sure?" "Of course, I'm sure come in." Paul was a little skeptical because this was the first time she had ever invited him in to stay for more than two hours for anything other than a gathering. He was beginning to wonder if her wall of not trusting anyone was falling. "Where would you like for me to sit your bags?" "Oh, just sit them in my room." He thought he was hearing things, so he asked her again and she repeated, "in my room." After a little thought she replied, "oh yeah you don't know where that is." "Top of the stairs center door down the hall." It wasn't apparent until that moment that everything in her life had been guarded from her heart to her house. Whenever she chooses to be intimate with Paul it was always at his place or one of the best hotels in Virginia. In the past two years they had been intimate approximately once a month because of her busy schedule and lack of trust. Nevertheless, Paul was always patient with her and it was only now since the death of Kimberly that she felt he was someone she could trust. Paul enjoyed the attention and security Silvia was forwarding him he just couldn't believe that after all this time she was finally coming around and allowing him to treat her the way that he desired. She called Paul into the study after he returned from placing the bags in her room. He had decided to look around a bit before he return to the first floor. Paul knew that one little step or word in the wrong direction would make her mood change therefore he always allowed her to set the mood and lead the way in all movements of their relationship. "Paul, I want you to see something." Paul walked into the study and glanced around the room. "Ok what is it?" "Baby look as she pointed to the wall." Mounted on the wall was a portrait of Paul and Silvia taken over two years ago when they first met and became friends. She had it mounted in a very nice bronze frame under a wall lamp. Paul looked at Silvia as she stared in his eyes and said, "I have more feelings for you than you could even know." Paul glared at her and said, "you could have fooled me." Silvia had decided at that very moment that she would allow Paul into her world even if it meant just long enough to earn her trust because he had certainly earned her love.

It was the beginning of spring a time when Silvia felt the joy of the seasons changing and she knew her favorite holiday was about to arrive. Christmas was the most joyous season in her life even before she had someone special to share it with. As early as September she would begin playing Christmas music and looking through old boxes for her favorite decorations. There was just something about the spring and winter season that would change her heart and mind regarding the way she perceived life. Silvia arrived from work one evening to find a letter from an old friend. The letter that arrived was from Malcolm, Silvia had completely forgot about missing the reunion up to that point and she wasn't sure what or why Malcolm would send her a letter instead of a correspondent card regarding the missed reunion date. Without hesitation Silvia opened the letter and began reading it.

Dear Silvia,

I really missed seeing you at the reunion. I realize that this letter may come as a surprise to you. However, I couldn't stop thinking about you ever since the last time I spoke with you over the phone. I hope by the time this letter reaches you all is well in your life. I am writing to you because since you were unable to make the reunion I was wondering if was possible to see you when I come to Virginia. I must conduct some business and I would love nothing more than to come and spend some time with you while I am there. I will call you before I get to your town. I hope to see you soon.

Your old friend,
Malcolm

Silvia loved Paul, and nothing could change that; not even Malcolm. She wondered if seeing Malcolm again after so many years could be very dangerous. Silvia stood holding the letter in her hand and daydreaming about Malcolm. He was her first love and she knew that the relationship they had would never really be extinguished by time nor distance. Upon the third call of her name by Mrs. Barnstine she finally snapped out of her daze and looked up. "Yes, Mrs. Barnstine." "Would you like for me to take the dogs out now," she stated in her heavy Russian accent? "Yes, Mrs. Barnstine," she replied. Just as she walked toward the bathroom to take a hot bubble bath the phone rang it was Paul. "Hi Babe, how are you?" "I am doing well; what about you?" "I am doing great." "I just received a letter for an old friend and he will be coming in town sometime next week." "I would like for you to meet him." "Him!?" Paul replied with a very inquisitive voice. "Yes, him he is an old friend from my childhood and a very nice guy." She could tell by his hesitation that he felt a little threaten at the thought of her seeing her long-time childhood friend nevertheless he replied; "sure, if you want me to meet him I will." "Great!" "I will call him later and find out the date and time that he will be arriving." Silvia loved Paul with all her heart and she just couldn't see him as being the jealous type and in the back of her mind she played it off as a cute little testosterone flexing. It was a nice warm breezy day at the airport when Malcolm arrived after he gathered his bags he headed over to the rental car counter to pick up his car. There were a few people in front of him waiting in line. They were waiting on their turn to give the two employees at the counter a hard time about the color, make, model, and size of the car of their choice which they would only possess for the next few days as they visited family members, vacation, or scurried off on business meetings. Upon his arrival to the counter Malcolm was so tired and suffering from the worst case of jet lag that he even agrees to the extra car insurance which no one hardly ever opted to get. He just wanted to get his rental car and check into his hotel. While driving to his hotel he decided to call Silvia to let her know that he had arrived safely and that after he took a nap he would call her to meet for lunch or dinner and drinks. Malcolm was a gentleman and would always seem to bring a smile to anyone's face that would have the pleasure of being in his company. As he began his journey he pushed the button on his Bluetooth and used the voice command call "Silvia Goshin." Upon the fourth ring Silvia answered the phone; "hello, hey now that is the sweetest voice I have heard today," he stated. With a glowing smile on her face she responded; "you are still a big flirt I see." Malcolm replied, "call it what you want." "I am speaking and calling it like I hear it." "So, are you in town?" "Yeah, my plane just got in I am headed over to my hotel to check in, take a shower and try to get a small nap in before I meet up with you if that is ok?" "Sure, that will be fine that will give us enough time to get ready." "Us," he replied? "Yes, us my boyfriend and I." "I would like for you to meet him his name is Paul and he is very nice matter of fact he kind of reminds me of you." "Then why not just settle for the real deal instead of messing with an old counterfeit version of me," he stated under his breathe? "What did you just say to me," she replied; as he laughed it off? "Nothing!" "I will call your later when I wake up from my nap." "Ok, I will see you later," she replied. It was about 5:45 pm by the time Silvia received a call from Malcolm. Paul was the greatest man alive in the eyes of Silvia and there was nothing that would come between her feelings for him. She had fallen head over heels in love with him. Yet, for some strange reason she could not understand why he was still and available man when she met him he just seemed so perfect and any woman would feel lucky to have him as a husband. When Malcom called Silvia around 5:45 pm he wanted to ensure that both she and Paul were still going to be able to meet with him. Silvia answered the phone and begin to converse with Malcom when her phone beep which signal she had received an incoming call. She asked for a brief hold from Malcom as she switched the line after viewing the screen to see that it was Paul calling. "Hey baby!" "Hey Paul," she replied. "I am so sorry, and I know it is late, but I am not going to be able to make it to dinner with you and your friend." "Please tell him I apologize." "Ok he is on the other line now, but what is going on?" "I have to work late on this project that has to be ready by the morning or my boss will kill me." "Ok, baby I understand," she replied. She then switched over to Malcom and informed him that it would just be the two of them to which Malcom was elated. Silvia arrived at the restaurant on time as always and shared a quick embrace with Malcom before sitting. "So, Ms. Goshin, tell me what has been going on in your world." "I am so glad that I get this moment to see that beautiful smile of yours again in person." "Let me stop you right there, you can pump the brakes with all that and save me the air fare with that flight full of bull." "What's up with you Malcom?" "You know I know better than this." "You didn't come here to discuss my smile or anything about my life." "What do you really want?" "Whoa slow down Sharp Tongue Tyrant." "I'm just trying to reconnect with an old friend is there anything wrong with that?" "You act like I asked you to go to bed." "I'm just trying to make conversation and pay you compliments." "Darn woman who peeped on your sandwich." "I'm sorry just been through a lot and I always have my B.S. radar on full blast." "Well I'm sorry for the past and the hurt you endured from it but I'm not him and I didn't do it." "I would never hurt you or cause you pain." "I would always fight for you, love, and care for you." "Just being your friend is enough for me I'm too grown to play games." "This is Malcom baby look at me!" With tears in her eyes it was obvious that Silvia still held on too much of the pain that plagued her heart from her previous relationships. She never sought any outside counseling or therapy to assist with her buried and self-healed pain. After dinner Malcom decided that he would keep the door open for Silvia to communicate with him. He knew that something was deeply rooted inside of her and because he wouldn't be in town for long he didn't want to pry. As they were eating dinner he expressed his love for her as her friend and that whenever and if ever she wanted or needed to talk he would be available. He made that abundantly clear when he stated that he would always be available whenever she needed him. "Silvia, come hell or high water; whenever you need me I am just a phone call away." "Whenever you pick up the phone I will be on the next thing smoking flying to be here." "Do you understand that?" "Yes, Malcom I know." "I apologize for snapping I just have so many different emotions plaguing my mind right now." "It's getting late and I must go I don't want Paul to worry." "I would love it if you would call me before you fly back home." "Ok, I will." "Tell Paul, thank you for allowing you to spend time with me tonight;" lucky mother trucker he muttered under his breath. "What did you say?" "Huh, um nothing just thank him for me."

After two and a half years Silvia was finally pouring her heart in soul into her relationship with Paul and nothing else in the world seemed to matter. In fact, Silvia began to feel the commitment itch coming on and playing sweet songs of fidelity in her ear. After the mid marking point of the third year of dating Paul decided he was no longer going to settle for just being a boyfriend. It was Easter Sunday and going out would not be unusual for them, so he decided he would use the holiday as a reason to take her out to their favorite restaurant and propose to her. He took her to their favorite restaurant and said he had a surprise for her when they were seated. He told her to close her eyes being the strong-minded woman she was she refused. "Just please close your eyes," he stated I have something for you. Again, she refused then he said, "you are not going to make this easy, are you?" He reached in his coat pocket bent down on one knee reached for her hand and in the presents of 100 or more people he proposed to her. With excitement and nervousness in her mind she said yes. Silvia was in utter shock and disbelief that she said yes. As tears rolled down her face she smiled and gave Paul a strong loving and compassionate kiss. The tears that Paul saw as joy was the unexplained fear she hid in her heart for their future together.

As she stared at the four-karat diamond platinum ring she wondered if she could really go through with marrying him. Could she really commit to the man she claimed to love? Will things change in their relationship after they said their I do's? Luckily her train of thought was broken by the entry of Janice her secretary with news of incoming files that required her attention. Silvia quickly responded; "thank you Janice." She turned quickly to halt Janice from her quick and purposeful stride back to her office. "Janice!" "Yes Ms. Goshin?" "Check my schedule and clear my week I have an emergency." With a puzzled looked on her face Janice asked if everything was ok. Silvia replied with a reassuring yes and she slowly closed the door to her office. She slowly picked up the phone to call Paul. Upon the fourth ring Paul answered. "Hello." "Hello, Paul I was calling to let you know that I am going to pack a small bag and leave for Colorado Springs tonight." "Tonight?" He stated with a panicked voice. "Yes, tonight," she replied. "I have some business to take care of and it can't wait." "Are you ok," he asked? "Yes, of course." "Do you need me to come with you?" "No baby I will call you once I arrive." "Ok as long as you are ok." "I am fine Paul." "I will call you in a few hours." As she hung up the phone Silvia wander if her next step was truly the right one. Silvia approached the gate to board the plane with dark eyes and an occupied mind filled with confusion and pain. She stopped short of the gangway and contemplated turning back in her mind she knew she had to go but her heart wanted to stay.

As she found her seat she retrieved a copy of the letter she wrote to Paul from her pocket.

Dear Paul,

I must apologize for my lack of candor regarding this situation. However, two months ago before you proposed to me I was at your apartment. I used the key you had given me to come over and surprise you. What I didn't know was that it was I who would receive the surprise. I walked inside and heard what I assumed were passionate moans coming from your bedroom door. I quietly opened the door and saw you and Jonathan in bed having sex. As bad as it hurt me to see you making love to another man I couldn't bring myself to respond or react. I knew the right thing to do was to walk away. These past seven weeks have been very difficult trying to keep everything together and not lose my mind. All I could think of was to find a way to come to grips with what I had seen in move on. I've had enough. I have been debating for weeks about what I should do. So, after contacting a friend and discussion my options. I decided to let the chips fall where they may. Enjoy your life. I pray that you will forever be happy.

Goodbye Silvia,

Upon her arrival to Colorado Silvia felt better about the decision she had made as soon as she saw him standing near the entry way of the corridor. "This is new for me and I am still not sure if this will work." He smiled and said; "it is ok we can take this one day at a time I know you have a lot of healing to do and we can take this as slow or as fast as you want." "Spending these last few months with you." Getting to know about the things you have endured just makes me want to take care of you even more." "I don't understand why you chose me as your psychiatrist when there are plenty reputable ones in your area." "I know that if Kimberly loved you they I can trust you." "Well thank you for putting your trust and faith in me." "I promise to take care of you and help you through this time in your life." "We will both help you through this." Kimberly turned around and saw Malcom standing behind her. She smiled and slowly walked towards him. They shared a long and passionate kiss. "I got you; you never have to deal with anything alone ever again," he said.

Cracked Bowl

"It's your fault that we didn't make the plane!" "You are always taking your time when it comes to important events Karen!" "What is your problem?" "Nothing just forget it!" "Let's go to the counter to see if we are able to catch the next flight out." "Boy I swear I must be dating the dumbest woman in Texas." "Augh!" Karen stood at the gangway with both her and Jahad's carry-on bags. Tears stung her eyes as she stood looking at the door close as the airline customer service representative told them they were too late. It wasn't the fact that they had missed their plane that made Karen feel indignant. It was the insulting manner in that Jahad responded to the situation. Karen felt as if it was impossible to please Jahad and she was constantly being criticized by him. They had arrived at the airport two minutes later than the designated time and had sadly missed their plane to Canada. Karen knew that it was not her fault they missed the plane but out of her love for Jahad she refused to remind him that it was in fact his fault they were late. He hadn't come over last night like he promised, and she had to wait for him to arrive this morning. It was he that showed up 45 minutes late to pick her up. Jahad and Karen were on their way to Canada to celebrate her family reunion. She believed with all her heart that Jahad intentionally made them late for the flight as a way of getting out of going to her family reunion. He would always forget important events when it came to the plans she made. However, if she was ever late to any of his preplanned events she would receive an ear full of insults and euphemisms used to describe both male and female genitalia. No matter how many times she heard the words; "you are in a toxic relationship" from her family and friends she held on to the hope that Jahad would change. When Jahad and Karen begin dating he was very charming and compassionate towards her. He traveled with her and did things that no man had ever done before. She loved and adored him and nothing anyone said regarding his past tainted the image of him. It was difficult for her to remove the blinders from her eyes. She heard his degrading words when he yelled them at her, but she felt he said those things out of love and passion. Upon rebooking for the next flight out of Texas which was due to leave in two hours Karen and Jahad sat down at gate D5 with their carry-on bags in the seat between them. He was checking his phone and she reading a memo from work she printed from her email. Her head was pounding, and it took all her strength to hold her head up and smile as if nothing was wrong. Jahad was so busy looking at text messages on his phone that he didn't notice the tall, milk chocolate complexed man who sat down next to Karen. "Are you alright," he asked? "I am ok," she responded. "I have a headache that's all." He quickly sprung to his feet, "are you allergic to any medications?" She looked up at him with a puzzled look. "No, why?" "I will be right back." When he returned he was holding a bottle of water and an individual package of Aleve. "Here take these, they might help." "The last thing you want is to have a headache before boarding a plane that will definitely making traveling a bit miserable." "Thank you Mr…" "The name is Shawn." "Thank you, Shawn." "Well, I gave you my name and you would be?" "Oh, I am sorry, my name is Karen." "Pleasure to meet you

Karen." "Canada your final destination or a connecting flight for somewhere else?" "We are headed to Canada for my family reunion." "We?" "Yes, my boyfriend and I." Karen pointed two seats over to Jahad who was now engulfed in a conversation on the phone. He was wearing his earbuds and had missed the introductions. "Does he have a name, or should I just refer to him as your boyfriend?" They both laughed as Karen stated; "sorry his name is Jahad." "You sure do apologize a lot for someone who has done nothing wrong." "I'm sorr…" "I mean… force of habit I guess." "I understand." By now her headache was subsiding. Karen was feeling better emotional and physically. As she turned to thank Shawn again she notices that Jahad had taken one of his earbuds out of his ear and is looking in her direction snapping his fingers. "Hello!" "I said did you remember to bring the gum?" "No, bae I thought you grabbed it." "Wow, so we have no gum." "Could you get up and go get some seeing as you are the one who forgot to bring it?" Completely embarrassed she looks over at Shawn and stands to her feet to walk over to the airport retail store. As she walks away Shawn watches her. Karen could feel his eyes as she glanced over her shoulder. She suddenly felt sexy and adore something she was no longer feeling in her relationship with Jahad. "Careful Karen," she said to herself as she walked on. "There is no way that you are feeling this man." "Besides you are in a committed relationship." Karen then dismissed what she was feeling and walked over to the counter to pay for the gum. She looked down at the magazine rack and noticed the title *7 Signs You Are in A Toxic Relationship.* She glanced back to see if Jahad or Shawn was watching as she grabbed the magazine and placed it on the counter. She asked for a bag to place her items in and begin to walk back towards the gate. Upon arriving she reached in the bag and pulled out the gum and gave one pack to Jahad and opened the other pack she bought for herself. By now she was accustomed to Jahad not sharing with her and didn't want any further embarrassment by asking him to. She placed the bag with the magazine in between the seat and carry-on bags. Shawn begins to laugh. "Not to be in your business but you don't have to hide it I read it myself when I was waiting in line earlier." "I used to be in one so I already know the signs." "I wasn't hiding it from you, she stated." "Oh," he says as he leans over winks and looks at Jahad. "From the looks of it you don't have to hide it from him either." Suddenly there is a loud crackle as the airline customer service representative announces that there are two available exit row seats if anyone is willing to exchange their seats and assist with exiting the plane in the event of an emergency. Karen quickly taps Jahad's shoulder. He removes one of his earbuds and yells. "What!" "Bae, we have an opportunity to get exit row seats." "Man get outta here with that!" "You go change your seat if you want." "Damn just give me a break!" Karen knows by now that the entire group of passengers have heard him, and she slowly walks to the desk. As she begins to ask the flight crew for one of the available seats she hears Shawn voice stating, "and I would like to have the other." Somehow knowing that Shawn would be in the seat next to her affirmed that the pleasantry of the flight would be certain. During the five-hour flight Shawn and Karen talked about life, their occupations and the inserts of the magazine regarding a toxic relationship. Shawn shared his experience, but Karen dared not to share her concerns for fear that if she did, she would be admitting that she was truly in an abusive and toxic relationship. As the plane landed Karen felt a bit of unhappiness come over her. She thanked Shawn and begin retrieving her and Jahad's carry-on bags from the overhead compartment. Shawn being the gentleman that he is, helped her by getting the bags down and carrying one of the bags as they disembarked. When they arrived at the end of the gangway he handed her the bag and their hands touched briefly as she looked into his eyes and thanked him for a pleasant plane ride. She could hear Jahad coming up the gangway complaining about how they would have and should have been there by now if they hadn't missed their flight earlier. Despite his usual banter Karen didn't care she just stood there watching as Shawn walked away. After retrieving their luggage and renting a car they travelled the 30 miles to the hotel that was hosting the family reunion. They checked in and immediately it was back to the phone for Jahad. He was texting and making calls as if he was an important business man away on a business trip. Karen made all the arrangements for the room, gathered the keys and the bellhop carried their luggage. When they arrived at the elevator Karen remembered she forgot to inform the desk clerk to let her family know of her arrival and room number. So, she tipped the bellhop gave Jahad one of the room keys and walked back to the desk. While waiting her turn in line she saw her cousins which were her uncle's daughters standing in line. They began talking about the exciting events that were planned for the weekend. Karen was so excited and vowed to have a wonderful time this weekend. As they hugged and discussed meeting up later Karen turned to walk towards the elevators to go to her room. There were several people waiting to get on the elevators and once the doors opened it was like a stampede. Karen wedged herself on one of the side walls and pushed the button for the 8th floor. The elevators stopped at each floor emptying out all but two people before reaching the 8th floor. In her haste to find a spot to get in the elevator Karen didn't notice the familiar face riding in the elevator with her. It wasn't until she arrived to the 8th floor that she turned to bid the remaining guest farewell that she saw the face of Shawn. "Hey, what are you doing here?" "Are you that is your best bet," he states. Karen grabs her magazine and closes the door. This time she decides to take the stairs to avoid the crowd in the elevator. Instead of going down she decides to walk up the four flights to the roof of the hotel where she will find peace, quietness and be alone. When she arrives to the top she finds more than she anticipates. There are chairs, tables and a small shaded area conducive to her needs. She is all alone and wonders if any of the other guest have found her little tranquil spot. She sits down in one of the chairs underneath the table umbrella. Two pages into her magazine and she hear a small soft psss from behind the tree. She completely ignores it because she is not about to allow anyone to take away her secret place of serenity. Again, she hears a psss. "Ok, who is that and what do you want?" "It's me Shawn." "What?" "Where are you and are you following me?" "No, but in about three minutes security will be up here to remove you!" "What?" "Wait, why I didn't do anything?" "Come over here quick they are coming!" He grabs her hand and quickly pulls her into a storage closet behind one of the trees. Just as security guards run through looking for whoever set off the silent alarm. They both peer through the cracked door as the security guards give the all clear over their radios and announce that the person must have left before they got there. Karen turns to face Shawn. "What is this place and why can't I be here?" "It is a secret place of tranquility for the owner of the hotel and his family." "That is the reason why there are alarms and cameras up here." "To keep hotel guest out." "Didn't you read the sign on the door that stated this area is not for hotel guest?" "No, I didn't see a sign I was reading my magazine." "So, why are you up here and how did you know I was here?" "Ok, you got me!" "My father owns a chain of hotels." "However, this one is mine, given to me by my father on my 25ᵗʰ birthday." "I had this spot created for me so that I could get away from all the craziness." "So, you lied." "You are not here for a fraternity reunion?" "Yes, I am, and I didn't lie." "I just didn't tell you I owned the hotel." "There was no reason to tell you, you didn't ask, and I didn't tell." "I told you my occupation was business and finance." "My hotel is a business and it gives me lots of finance." They both laugh. "Ok, smarty pants." "Now let me out of here." She pushes on his chest as he grabs her face and kisses her. She slowly opens her mouth and allows him to trace her lips with his tongue. She grabs the back of his head with both hands drawing him in as places one hand on the side of her face and the other in the small of her back. Gently and slowly he continues kissing her passionately as their tongue danced softly and intertwind. "What are we doing," she says with a smothered voice? "Shawn!" "What are we doing?" "I don't know but this feels so damn good," he responds. "Shawn, we can't, not like this." "I am with someone and I love him." "I know and I apologize." Although they are both in agreeance that what they are doing is wrong passion has consumed them and they just can't stop. Suddenly Shawn is fully erect, and he can no longer hide the desire growing within him. He takes a step back and looks at Karen. "We can't." "Not like this." "I know," she responds. They both agree and just as quickly as it started it was over. Karen composed herself kissed Shawn on the lips and walked away. Shawn needing more time to adjust waited five more minutes before leaving the closet. Karen felt overwhelmed with guilt as she entered the room. She saw Jahad lying on the bed. She sat down next to him and rubbed his back to wake him. He rolled over slowly. "I hope you went and got your crap together," he says. Karen looks at him with regretful eyes and states; "I need to tell you something." Shawn not interested snaps, "this is what I am talking about you always do this crap!" "Every time we go somewhere you always get emotional."

"Wanna talk about feelings and what's on your mind." "I get sick of hearing this crap Karen." "Grow a back bone." "Damn!" "Jahad, I haven't said what I need to tell you." "Hell, you don't have to!" "I can feel you thinking it." "I will be glad when this stupid gathering ya'll having is over!" I am ready to go home." "I got other important stuff to do." "Dumb ass family reunion!" "Meeting a bunch of old ass people talking bout remember when in shit." "Augh!" "Get off the bed sit on the floor or something I need to finish sleeping." "Man, I can't stand you sometimes Karen." "You like a damn nat!" He then begins mocking her "oh, we need to effectively communicate our feeling to one another Jahad." "I think we ought to discuss some things Jahad." "Oh, Jahad wouldn't it be nice if we went on a trip to la la I don't give a damn!" Karen didn't know whether to be filled with rage or hurt either way she was tired from the plane ride and the verbal abuse and just wanted to rest. She pulled the spare blanket and pillow from the closet and laid down on the couch. As she lay there she thought about Shawn and how he made her feel. She replayed the images in her mind. While playing the images in her mind she peacefully fell asleep with a smile on her face. While sleeping Karen heard faint sounds of heavy breathing and soft moans. She could hear what she thought was Jahad's voice saying, "shut up for you wake her dumb ass up." She slowly opened her eyes and noticed that Jahad was having sex with another woman. When he noticed Karen watching he told her it was all her fault he had to get it from someone else because she was sleeping and he wasn't about to wait on her to wake up to give him sex. Karen jumped up and ran out the door holding her chest. Jahad had done some low and hurtful things to her but this was the last straw. Karen went down stairs and asked for another room. She was informed that there were no other rooms available. She thought about calling her mother or her sister and down." "Tell him there is a problem with the key and I will grab my things and be out before he comes back up." "What about the family reunion?" "Knowing him he will leave the hotel before he shows up there." "Ok I will personally go to the room and escort him to the front desk so that there isn't any confusion." Shawn goes to the room and knock on the door he gets no answer. He knocks again and still no answer. He inserts his master key. There he finds Jahad pumping away like a teenager getting laid for the first time. Jahad jumps to his feet. "Hey man, what the hell are you doing?" "Sorry sir I knocked several times and got no answer, Shawn states." "There is a problem with the room keys and it needs to be attended to immediately." "I am kinda in the middle of something which I know you can see." "Well sir, I sure can." "However, you still need to come to the front desk now otherwise we will not be able to rectify the situation later." "Ok, man damn!" "Hey, don't go anywhere I'll be right back," Jahad states to the young lady he was taking to pound town. "I apologize for the inconvenience sir, but this is not the young lady who rented this room." "Am I correct?" "So, What?" "Well she can not remain in the room while you are not present." "Company policy states that either one or both occupants must be present in the room when outside guest are in the room due to liability concerns." "Really dude?" "Come on baby get dressed we gonna finish this in a minute." As they all proceed out the door and to the elevator Karen waits until they are out of sight and quickly goes in the room. They had not been there very long, so her bags were still packed and all she had to do was grab what belonged to her. She grabbed her things and ran to the elevator. She bumped into her sister coming out of the elevator. "Hey girl where are you running off to like a run away slave?" "What?" "No where just switching rooms." "There is a problem with our room and Jahad just went down to go get the keys to our new room." "Oh, ok that would explain it, because I just saw him on the elevator with some man and a chic." "For a second I thought he was playing you." They both laughed. "Ok, Karen says as the elevator stops on the 9th floor I will talk with you all in a about an hour at the meet and greet." "Ok Sis love you." "I love you too," she responds. Karen walked to the door of room 915. She inserted the key Shawn had given her. She wasn't sure what to expect but she knew whatever lie ahead had to be better than what was in her past. The room was astonishing. It was bigger than any room she had ever rented or seen at a hotel. It was filled with elegant furniture, beautiful art work and upscale décor. The room was breathtaking. She placed her bags on the floor and thought about exploring each room until her most vexing attribute kicked in. She decided to sit and wait on the couch knowing well that she was a guest of Shawn and she would not want him to think she was there with alterative motives. She became very passive and quiet. She found a place on the sofa and there she remained for 20 minutes until Shawn appeared. He came and sat down next to her on the couch. "Is there something wrong?" "Are you ok," he asked? "Everything is fine I was just waiting for you to tell me which room would be mine for the weekend." "I don't want you to alter your plans for me." "I surely wasn't about to go snooping around your place." Shawn grabbed her hands and looked at her in the eyes as he spoke and said, "you are my plans for the weekend." "After seeing how that man treats you, you deserve nothing but the best if only just for this weekend." "Pick which ever room you want, order whatever you want and do whatever you want." "Don't worry about a thing charge anything you want to the room." "They have orders downstairs to be at your beckoning call." "Shawn why are you doing this?" "I don't know you and you don't know me." "I don't have to know you, but I know your heart." "I can see your hurt and I can feel your pain." "Where you are now I was three years ago." "It was only after I realized that love doesn't hurt you or try to destroy you that I was able to find myself and what makes me happy." "I promised myself to never be afraid to love again." "I asked God to send me a clear sign of the woman he wants me to love." "A woman who will need me as much as I need her." "Even if you are not that person I want you to know what it feels like to be loved and cared for this weekend." Karen was full of emotions as tears streamed down her face she wept like she had never wept before. Shawn embraced her, and she was comforted. He kissed the top of her head and brushed away her tears. Karen looked up at Shawn with her light brown eyes and kissed Shawn softly on the lips. Shawn reciprocated her passion. He then slowly kissed her neck and went down to her breast. She cupped his ears as she exhaled. He moved ever so slowly back to her mouth and then to her ears. "Tell me what you want me to do for you Ms. Karen." "Have your way Shawn," she responded. Shawn lifted her off the couch and carried her to the master bedroom where he slowly disrobed her. Although, Karen had an impeccable body her insecurities allow her to be very timid with exposing her nakedness. Shawn forbade her to cover up and he affirmed her beauty by stating, "you are so beautiful baby." Her gave the shower command to turn on warm water as he disrobed and led her to the shower. He lathered her body with soap and then lathered himself. He pressed his body against hers and picked her up allowing the soapy sensation of their bodies to generate heat and passion. As the water cascaded down their bodies he placed her on the shower bench and kneeled until he was on all fours. He opened her legs and told her to remain in that position as he slowly traced her with his tongue. As he vigorously vibrated his tongue back and forth he inserted two fingers. Within several minutes she climaxed. He then pulled her from the bench, turned her face down interlock his legs with hers and bent her back on top of him as he lifted slightly from the shower floor with each thrust. Karen felt as if she was riding a horse bareback and she was enjoying every minute of it. He then commanded the shower off and he lifted her and placed her on the bathroom counter top there he gentle tied her hands together and whispered, "the safe word is *cured*." He begins tasting her nectar. Softly sucking and vibrating his tongue and occasionally providing long hard thrusts of his throbbing erection as he sucks her fingers. Karen had never been so stimulated in her life. She had never had a man bring her to the moment of ecstasy. In the past she had always just went through the motions and waited until the very unsatisfying sexual session was over. She would provide and occasional oh ah, oh this feels so good and yes baby to encourage her mate. On occasions she would sneak in the bathroom or lie in bed and pleasure herself. She was embarrassed to share with anyone that she had discovered on her own how to have an orgasm. No man up until this point had ever lasted long enough or knew what they were doing well enough to make her reach her peak. She had heard stories from her girlfriends about the tantalizing details of their erotic moments with their mates but never had she experienced her own personal gratifying moment. She thought that something was wrong with her because she had never personally experienced it. It wasn't until she read a book written by a well renown sex therapist who explained that most men don't know how to please a woman sexually because they don't understand how the vagina works and they never take the time to listen or learn. No one woman is the same and what works for some women may not work on others. The male ego interferes with the needed knowledge to satisfy a woman. When a woman attempts to explain to a man what is sexually pleasing to her. He often misconstrues it as criticism. When in reality all the woman is saying let me show you what works for me. By now Shawn is having a French kissing lesson with her vagina. He unties her hands and lowers her to the floor exhausted she thought he was finished until he bends her over gently but with forceful pushing her head in the sink as if he is about to wash her hair and begin thrusting her from behind. She wasn't quite sure as to why he was counting whenever he engaged her body and she never bothered to ask. Shawn was counting how many thrust and licks it took to before she climaxes. He later explained that knowing her point of climax was a turn on and it enticed him more to please her in ever way. After 46.7 minutes of pleasing Karen's body in a way that had never happened there was a knock on the door. "Mr. Shawn!" "Are you in there?" Shawn opened the door in his bathrobe. "Yes, Carter." "What is wrong?" "Sir, we have a complaint that one of the hotel guests has gone missing sir." "What?" "Who?" "A Ms. Karen Novack Sir." "What?" "Wait!" "Carter who reported her missing?" "Her fiancé sir, Mr Jahad." "Carter, Ms. Karen is not missing." He pulls the door back exposing Karen sitting on the couch in her bathrobe. "She is here." "Very well sir, what should I convey to Mr. Jahad?" By now Karen was interjecting. "No need Carter, I will be down in a few minutes to meet my family in the Shore room for the meet and greet." "If Mr. Jahad wishes to speak with me he can speak with me there in 20 minutes." Karen didn't know what the future would hold for her, but one thing was for sure she was not going back to being treated the way she had been for the past year in a half by Jahad. After being with Shawn she had all the motivation she needed to move forwarded. She now understood what her grandmother had once explained to her about broken sugar bowls. A sugar bowl is filled with good sweet sugar. If the bowl is whole and solid the sweetness will

About the Author

Larouna Pinckney-Maybin grew up in the Sunshine State (Florida). She has a large family; she is one of 21 children from her mother and one of eight children from her father. She is the mother of three beautiful children. She enjoys reading, listening to music, singing, mentoring and writing. She has written and published two books (self-published) titled: *The Force of Life's Confessions* and *My Blessings, My Stacks, and My Life*. She continues to write for enjoyment and publish books to leave a legacy of inspiration for her children. She finds joy in giving to others. Her prayer is to one day be able to give to others as much love, inspiration and joy as she has been blessed to have in her life.